OTHERLAND

LOUIE STOWELL

nosy
crow

First published in the UK in 2021 by Nosy Crow Ltd
The Crow's Nest, 14 Baden Place,
Crosby Row, London SE1 1YW

Nosy Crow and associated logos are trademarks and/or registered
trademarks of Nosy Crow Ltd

Text © Louie Stowell, 2021
Cover and chapter opener illustrations © George Ermos, 2021

The right of Louie Stowell to be identified as the author of this
work has been asserted.

ISBN: 978 1 78800 046 8

A CIP catalogue record for this book is available from
the British Library

Printed and bound in Great Britain by Clays Ltd, Elcograf S.p.A.
Typeset by Tiger Media

Papers used by Nosy Crow are made from wood grown
in sustainable forests.

MIX
Paper from
responsible sources
FSC® C018072

3 5 7 9 10 8 6 4 2

www.nosycrow.com

*To Margot, who was never stolen by fairies but
who might be one herself, I can't be sure.*
L.S.

Prologue

Two babies are born in the same hospital. Two tiny voices cry out, then fall silent. Their hearts stutter. Their lungs stop filling. People run. Machines bleep. A parent screams.

After an eternity, air returns to the tiny lungs. The little hearts are beating. The parents sob happy tears. All is right with the world.

Except...

A rip in the universe has been torn, from our world to another. And someone is watching. She knows, if she waits long enough, the hole will grow. She knows, if she watches closely enough, she'll find her moment and claim her prize.

Time rolls on, until one day she sees the flames, and she knows: it's now.

Those babies are going to wish they'd never been born.

1
Hurricane Myra

Myra's mum gave her hand a squeeze and smiled at her from beneath her bright-red clown nose. "Happy deathday, Myra," she said.

"Thanks, Ma!" said Myra. She gave her mum a big toothy grin and tried to feel excited. They were walking to Myra's joint birthday party, which she had every year with her not-exactly-friend Rohan. Spending time with perfect Rohan always set her on edge. Standing next to him felt like turning up to school in your dirty pyjamas when everyone else is wearing perfectly ironed white clothes.

She scuffed her neon wellingtons along the ground as they passed the kebab shops and key cutters of the long, litter-strewn high street where she lived, and gave herself a talking-to. *It's my birthday*, she thought. *It's a happy day. Think happy thoughts.* But the gloom kept spreading through her, like that damp patch in the corner of the living room.

She looked at her mother and made herself smile again. It felt like trying to control a sad, wet puppet, only the puppet was her face. Her mother smiled back.

"Aren't birthdays amazing?" she said.

Myra nodded. "Amazing."

To celebrate Myra's birthday, her mother was dressed as a clown and holding a large armful of red helium balloons. It was one of her more restrained fancy-dress outfits.

As they walked through the brightly lit shopping centre, hand in hand, Myra's mum got a lot of dirty looks from passers-by but Myra didn't care. They were just jealous that they didn't have their own clown.

She looked up at her mother with a chest full of pride. Bridget Duffy was such a big personality, sometimes Myra felt a little squished beside her. That meant she just needed to puff herself up and be as much fun as physically possible, didn't it?

Myra was dressed in her birthday best, with a flower behind each ear and her curly brown hair loose and wild. She wore a bright-green ballet tutu, a neon-yellow T-shirt reading NOW PANIC AND FREAK OUT and a pair of luminous-green wellingtons. As she walked beside her mum, she had a moment's worry that she should have worn a fancy-dress costume too.

Worries aren't for birthdays, remember? she told herself. It was one of her mother's many sayings, along with *No one likes a whiner* and *Never trust a Virgo.*

"Rohan's part of town is so boring, isn't it?" said her mum. "It's like a morgue round here."

They were turning on to the street where Rohan lived. It was lined with trees and everything was quiet and calm and smelled faintly of roses. The street where Myra lived was a car-clogged main road, and it smelled mostly of exhaust and chips.

"So boring," agreed Myra. The silence on the road made her thoughts feel loud.

"What's in the bag, sweetie?" asked her mother, apparently only just noticing that Myra was carrying a rucksack.

"It's a surprise!" said Myra mysteriously.

"That's my girl!" chuckled her mother, handing her a balloon. "Let it go and watch it soar!" she suggested.

Myra let go of the string and the balloon floated away into the sky. She wondered what that would feel like, being so light and so high.

Soon they reached Rohan's neat, freshly painted house and Myra rang the bell. A millisecond later, she reached out to ring it again in case they hadn't heard, but the door swung open. Rohan was standing just inside, like he'd been waiting there.

"Hello," said Rohan. He looked worried.

Then again, Rohan always looked worried. He was five foot five inches of worry in human form. His black hair was gelled up, contributing at least one of those inches. Myra wasn't sure how it was physically possible for hair to look worried, but Rohan's did. His dark eyes were wide, looking at Myra like you might look at a bomb ticking down to the last second of its timer.

Myra thought he looked like he was dressed for a funeral. And not in a fun, morbid, "it's my deathday" way. He had on a dark-blue shirt and darker-blue trousers. The only hint of colour was his tie, which was red. But also: it was a *tie*. He was wearing an actual tie. It made him look like a grown-up who'd been on the wrong end of a shrink-ray.

"HELLO!" said Myra, at capital-letter volume. "HAPPY DEATHDAY TO US! SCREAM!" She followed the word "scream" with a proper, ear-piercing scream, holding her hands on either side of her face. Making an entrance was important, especially at a party.

Rohan covered his ears until she'd finished. He looked up and down the street, checking if anyone was nearby, then beckoned, hissing, "Please come in?"

"Yeah! Let's get this party started!" said Myra's mum,

pumping the air with her frilly-sleeved arm. "WOO!"

"Er, hello, Mrs Duffy," said Rohan, blinking up at the clown in his doorway. "You know it's just going to be us and a few aunties this year, right? Because of last year…?" Rohan tailed off, looking at Myra then looking away.

Myra's stomach dropped remembering that. Well, she hadn't forgotten so much as buried the knowledge under her happy thoughts.

The Myra and Rohan joint party was traditional. Myra and Rohan were born in the same hospital, on the same night, and both of them had died after they were born. It had only been for a minute, and they'd recovered completely thanks to some very quick-thinking doctors and nurses. It was a medical miracle that the two families got together to celebrate once a year.

Myra thought the miracle might be a cursed one, given that something always went wrong at these parties.

The things that went wrong were never exactly Myra's fault, unless you were fussy and defined "her fault" as "happening because of something she'd done".

Last year had been worse than usual. She'd opened the door so enthusiastically to the magician that he'd ended up with a broken hand, and his only trick had been turning himself into a hospital patient. There had also been an incident with some superglue and Rohan's cousin's hair, which led to an emergency hairdresser visit.

Her mum hadn't punished her, luckily. Myra's mum never told her off or gave her punishments of any kind. It wasn't part of her parenting philosophy. "I don't like to limit my Myra," she liked to say. "I want her to find her own limits."

However, it turned out that Rohan's mum wasn't keen on allowing Myra to find her own limits while under her roof. So this year Myra had been sent a list of rules.

No matches

No superglue

No opening the front door

No fun

OK, that last one wasn't strictly on the list. But it seemed to be what Rohan's parents were getting at. What kind of party has *rules*?

Rohan looked up and down at Myra's mother's clown wig, patchwork trousers and full facepaint with a doubtful expression.

"So, yeah … there won't be any kids," he said.

Myra thought it was about right that Rohan didn't count himself as a child.

"So what?" said Mrs Duffy. "The smaller the party, the

more effort we have to put into making it fun, don't we?" Her voice was slightly muffled by a big red nose pinching her actual nose. She reached to her clown lapel and a jet of water squirted out of a plastic flower, right into Rohan's face. "Happy deathday, sweetheart!" she chuckled.

"Thank you?" said Rohan, wiping his eye and flattening himself to the wall to let them past. Myra thought he stayed flattened longer than he needed to, as though he trusted the wall more than he trusted Myra and her mother.

'Balloon?" said Myra's mum, holding one out for Rohan to take.

"I ... why not," said Rohan.

"Later, we can inhale the helium and talk in tiny ant voices!" suggested Myra's mum.

Rohan made a horrified face. "That's very bad for you!"

Myra's mum shrugged. "Is it? Ah! Hello, little one! Give Aunty Bridget a squish!" She held out her arms as Rohan's little sister, Shilpa, came toddling along, giggling to herself.

But, seeing the clown in her hallway, Shilpa squealed and ran to Rohan instead, grabbing on to his trouser leg.

Myra thought her mum looked sad for a moment. But that was impossible. Myra's mum was never sad at parties.

"Awww, she loves her brother," was all Bridget Duffy said.

Rohan stroked Shilpa's dark curly head gently. The little girl was wearing Spider-Man pyjamas and yawning her face off. "Not sleepy!" she said to Rohan. "Party games!"

"You need to have your nap first," said Rohan. "Then you can play party games."

"Party games!" repeated Shilpa excitedly. "Now?"

"Later. Sleepy time now. Shall I sing you a lullaby? Your favourite?"

"'K," said Shilpa, nestling into his leg like a koala clinging to a tree. Then, just in case anyone was under the impression she was going to take any of this lying down, she added, "Play now!"

"Shh, later," said Rohan. He tried to look stern, but as Shilpa looked up at him with her big dark eyes, he melted and gave her a tickle.

"PLAYYYYY!" she shrieked, then dissolved into giggles of joy.

Rohan's mother came downstairs just then, smelling of perfume and looking film-star elegant. Myra was half convinced she wasn't a real person, but instead some kind of hologram. She wore a very pretty green dress with a wispy, shiny scarf and everything about her seemed to glow with perfection.

Rohan hurriedly picked up Shilpa and tried to shhh her out of her giggle fit.

"Priyamvada!" said Mrs Duffy. She looked down awkwardly at her clown costume for a moment, then back up at Rohan's mum, her smile faltering slightly under her clown nose. "You look gorgeous!"

"Thank you!" Rohan's mum replied. "Though now I feel underdressed. LOVE the clown costume!"

Myra's mum beamed at that.

"Would you like some chai while we wait for the food to be ready?" Rohan's mum went on.

Myra could smell the food. Spiced warmth and fresh bread.

Myra's mum honked her red nose, which meant she was indeed interested in some chai, and the adults filed off into the kitchen. Myra went to follow them but Myra's mother shook her head.

"You go and play," she said. "I need some grown-up time!"

Myra swallowed. The fresh-baked smells soured in her nostrils. "Let's do something fun!" she said to Rohan, who was holding a struggling Shilpa.

"I'm going to put her down for her nap, then we can play Thronehammer," said Rohan, hoiking his sister up further into his arms. She giggled and pulled his hair down over his eyes. "It's set up under the awning, in case it rains. Shilpa, don't do that. I need to go upstairs and I can't see."

That made Shilpa giggle and mess with his hair even more as he carried her upstairs.

"Rohaaaaa!" she cooed. "Rohaaaa! Not sleep! Not sleep!"

"Come on, I don't want to drop you," said Rohan, wrestling Shilpa away from his face as he mounted the stairs.

Myra smiled. Shilpa never did what she was told, and Myra appreciated that in a person, even a very small person.

"Can't she play for a bit?" asked Myra, thinking Shilpa would probably be more fun than Rohan.

"Play Myra!" agreed Shilpa, holding out her fat arms to Myra.

"No!" Rohan was halfway up the stairs. "You're not helping, shh!"

"Fine!" said Myra, feeling a slight sting, but pushing it down. *This is going to be fun, remember. Nothing can stop it being fun. It doesn't matter that Mum doesn't want to hang out with me. She's had all morning with me, hasn't she? So other people should get to be with me too!*

OK, so there weren't any other people nearby. But Rohan would be back down soon. She headed out to the garden, with her bag on her shoulder. It contained precious things and could not be let out of her sight. The bag was covered in badges. One of them read, "Death to the Patriarchy!" One said, "Save the animals, eat plants!" and another said, simply, "Puppies!" Myra had broad-ranging tastes, but was consistent in her love for exclamation marks on everything. They just made words look more exciting!

Myra sat down in one of the garden chairs, with her Very Important Bag at her side, and surveyed the Thronehammer board like a general preparing for battle.

The pieces were laid out neatly, with the dice beside the board and the rule book in pride of place. Myra loved all the characters in the game, and the art on the box. It showed a dwarf, and an elf, and a human warrior battling a giant spider. The reality of the game never quite lived up to the art. It was a role-playing game, where you pretended to be fantastical characters, go on quests, and fight monsters. She was happy with all of that, but there were so many rules!

No eating magical food!

No using iron weapons with a fairy character!

No carrying on fighting when you've taken 900 hit

points after a particularly enthusiastic solo attack on a troll…

…and Rohan was a real stickler about it all. For instance, she didn't see why she wasn't allowed to cast a ninth-level spell with a fourth-level wizard character, but he'd go ballistic when she tried it.

She'd be like, "But what if I'm feeling EXTRA powerful today? KABAM! Fireball!" This made Rohan start hopping from foot to foot with anxiety.

There was a scraping noise, and the window to the kitchen opened. Sounds of plates and bowls and cups emerged, and various aunties offering better ways to do things, until Mrs Patel suggested they go and lay the table.

Myra turned her attention back to the board, deciding which character she wanted to be today. Rohan had a ninth-level wizard he'd been playing for the last year, but she'd managed to kill all her characters so far, except a berserker. The good thing about berserkers was that when you rushed in without a plan to attack the enemy, that was actually what you were supposed to do, and as a result, her Thorag the Foolhardy character wasn't dead. Yet.

Adult voices drifted boringly out of the kitchen.

"How's the business going?" Mrs Patel was asking.

"Oh, you know," said Myra's mum. "Slowly. I'm not

sure people are quite ready for healing yoghurt. And it's so hard, juggling the business and looking after Myra."

At the sound of her own name, her ears pricked up.

"I'm sorry, that sounds hard," said Mrs Patel. "I don't know how you do it."

"What they don't tell you when you have a kid is how hard it is to get anything done. Love her, but she never stops talking when I'm trying to concentrate."

The words were like nails on a chalkboard, but inside her ribcage. Myra gritted her teeth.

"Well, if you ever want her to come here to give you a break, just say the word," said Mrs Patel.

"Dangerous words, my friend. You might find I've packed a trunk and Myra's living with you before too long!" laughed Myra's mother.

Myra didn't want to hear any more of that. She knew she cramped her mum's style, but she didn't want to listen to her saying it out loud. She got up suddenly, knocking her bare knees against the Thronehammer table and scattering pieces all over the patio.

The voices in the kitchen suddenly hushed, and someone reached out to close the window.

Myra looked down at the fallen pieces, biting her lip. Rohan was going to be angry. He spent ages setting up

Thronehammer games and always did it so carefully and perfectly. She got down on her knees and started to rescue the meticulously painted little warriors and wizards, and the dice and the monsters. She placed them back on the board, but she couldn't remember where they'd been to begin with. She put a cave troll in the tavern where they started the game, instead of somewhere predictable like a dungeon. Why not start the game with a bang?

In fact, why not start the party with a bang? She glanced back at her bag. When she'd packed it, she hadn't been sure she'd actually go through with it. But now … she'd show her mum she wasn't just a drag. She could be fun to be around, and not just in the way!

Just then, Rohan came out. He stared at the board with horror. "What did you do?"

Myra shrugged. "I moved things around a bit. But let's play Thronehammer later. I've got an idea for something much more exciting. Come on!"

She snatched up her bag full of precious things and beckoned him to follow.

"What?" asked Rohan. "Where are you going?" He trotted to catch up with her, looking like he'd swallowed a bag of spiders, and every one of those spiders was having an emotional crisis inside him. What did he have to worry about? This was a party! And it wasn't like his mum thought *he* was a dead weight. No, he was Mr Never Naughty, Mr Perfect, Captain Can Do No Wrong!

"Keep up!" she said, and disappeared into the damp bushes that sectioned off the main part of the garden from the bit with the fish pond at the back. Rohan's parents' garden was huge. He and Myra used to play that there were monsters living back there when they were little, except Myra wasn't playing. She had fully believed they were real, and used to leave food out for them. The local rats and foxes LOVED that. Rohan's parents did not.

Myra opened her bag, glancing up at the sky. It might rain any moment, so it was now or never.

By the time Rohan reached her, she was lining up fireworks, sticking each one into the ground, then tying a string between the blue paper bits at the bottom. She smiled as she did it. This was going to be amazing.

"What are you doing?" asked Rohan.

As Myra stuck the last firework in the ground, she turned to him, dusting off her hands. She was excited to share her incredibly clever and very scientific plan. "I thought, since it's daytime, the fireworks won't show up very well against the sky. So I thought I'd connect a few together so they'd be more…" She gestured. "BOOM! Shall I light them or do you want to?"

"But…" said Rohan. "You're not supposed to have matches."

"Aha!" She pulled the cigarette lighter out of her pocket and waved it at him in triumph. "I'm not going to use *matches* to light them. See! I'm totally following the rules!"

"I don't think the no-matches rule was strictly about matches…" Rohan sighed. "I think the point was that you weren't supposed to set things on fire. You know, like the time you set all my birthday cards on fire trying to light the candles on the cake?"

"But 'no setting things on fire' wasn't what your mum SAID, was it?" Myra shook her head. He wasn't getting it. "It said no matches. How am I supposed to obey stuff she hasn't said? I'm not psychic. Even though my mum says it does run in the family…" Myra flicked the lighter with a loud SNICK. She bent down and lit the string at one end of the uber-firework chain.

Myra wasn't entirely sure what happened next.

There were definitely some very loud bangs, flashes, crashes and a high-pitched whining that sounded like a devil escaping from hell and entering a dance contest against a cannon.

Then she looked up to discover that the shed was on fire.

Adult screaming came from the house. Running footsteps. More shouting. A crying toddler.

"Oops," said Myra. She frowned. "I didn't mean to do that."

"The shed, Myra," said Rohan. He ran his fingers through his hair, looking as terrified as a hamster at a cat show. "You set fire to the shed."

"Yeah," said Myra. She started feeling a bit glum. Then, realising something, a smile flashed out, and she made a triumphant gesture at the blazing structure. "But at least I didn't break the rules!"

Beside her, Rohan put his head in his hands and panicked, energetically.

2

Happy birthday, everything's on fire

Rohan's dad had reached the bottom of the garden and was staring in horror at the fire. "PRI, CALL THE FIRE BRIGADE!" he yelled back at his wife, who was already dialling on her mobile.

"Oh my," said Myra's mum, arriving at her daughter's side. "The flames… It's going up VERY quickly, isn't it!"

"It is," Myra agreed. She glanced awkwardly at Rohan and his parents, and his very scared-looking aunties. "I'm…" She tailed off. She didn't want to say sorry, because admitting something was your fault before anyone blamed you for it seemed hasty. Like going to prison before you got arrested.

"I'll go and get the hose!" said Rohan's dad. "Kids, get back to the house. Stay with your sister, Rohan. Keep her safe! Would everyone else get back inside!"

"Yes, we have a fire in the garden, it's the shed," Rohan's mum was saying to the person on the other end.

"Our address is…"

"Should I get everyone cake?" suggested Myra's mum. "That might take our minds off it." She'd taken off her clown nose and was staring dreamily at the fire. "Or marshmallows to toast? How about some marshmallows, love?" she asked Myra, a little absently.

Myra did fancy some marshmallows, but part of her wished her mum was a bit more worried about the fire. Not that she was a killjoy, it was just that the flames were really quite big now and her mother wasn't even trying to get her to move back.

Finally, Rohan spoke, breaking out of his horrified daze.

"Let's go," he said, grabbing Myra's arm and pointing to the house.

With a reluctant look over her shoulder, Myra joined him in trotting back to the house. A child was crying over the crackling flames. *Must be Shilpa*, thought Myra. "Can't I stay to see what happens?" asked Myra.

"GET INSIDE! BOTH OF YOU! WE WILL TALK ABOUT THIS LATER!" roared Rohan's dad, in a voice that really wasn't very birthday-ish. Myra shook off Rohan and slunk back towards the house. Her throat was feeling dry and scratchy from the smoke, and her eyes were watering.

When Rohan and Myra reached the house, they went upstairs. On the landing, Rohan stopped before opening the door to his sister's bedroom. "Myra, you REALLY can't keep doing this stuff," he said. "Like … you could have actually killed someone this time."

Myra looked at her green-wellington-clad feet. Her eyes welled up. She wasn't crying, though. It was the smoke. "I just wanted the party to be exciting…" She tailed off and pointed to the door with her thumb. "She's stopped crying. Maybe we should go back and help the adults?"

"I think you've probably helped enough for the day," snapped Rohan.

"FINE!" Myra snapped back. The watery eyes were gone. Now she felt fiery. "I know YOU'RE perfect in every way," she yelled. "But you don't have to rub it in my face."

"Perfect? I'm definitely not perfect, I'm just not a pyromaniac!" Rohan was yelling now too. He didn't look worried like he usually did. He looked furious. Myra didn't like it. "Why do you have to ruin EVERYTHING? Every birthday ends up a mess because of you!" he was yelling. "Remember the Great Baby Snake Escape on our eighth birthday! Or last year's triumph when you broke someone's hand then superglued my cousin's hair to her face!"

"I was just trying to make it shiny like in the adverts!" objected Myra. "It's not my fault that adverts give us unrealistic expectations of beauty standards like my mum says!"

"What about my cousin's *realistic* expectation not to be glued to herself?" shot back Rohan. Then his expression softened ever so slightly. "Look, can't we just have *one* birthday where you don't create some giant mess for me to clear up?"

"You don't have to clear it up!" said Myra, biting her lip to stop a sob belching up her throat. "The fire brigade are going to do that!"

"AAAARGH! I can't talk to you right now! Not without wanting to kill you!" Rohan made an exasperated snort and opened the door to his sister's bedroom. "I'm going to go and spend some time with someone a bit more mature than you. MY EIGHTEEN-MONTH-OLD SISTER!"

He stomped into Shilpa's bedroom and over to her cot, where she was napping. Myra hovered in the doorway, knowing she wasn't welcome in there, but not quite willing to go downstairs and face adult rage either. Rohan's dad had just shouted at her, sure, but what she was dreading was Rohan's mum. Her Not-Angry-Just-Disappointed face was worse than any shouting. It was like having your soul sliced open with red-hot lasers of disappointment.

Better to stay in here, where it was safe.

Or was it?

Over Rohan's shoulder, Myra saw a wisp of pinkish smoke rise from the bedclothes of Shilpa's cot. She felt a sudden jolt of fear. Had the fire spread in here?

"Oh no!" Rohan rushed to the cot, clearly seeing the smoke too.

Myra was by his side in a second. She looked down into the cot.

Little Shilpa was staring up at them with her deep-brown eyes, completely not on fire. Her curly black hair was messy on the pillow, as usual when she was snuggled in bed. Her brown skin glowed with healthy not-on-fireness. She was as quiet as a mouse, just looking up from beneath her thick lashes, perfectly unhurt and unbothered by all the commotion outside.

Maybe the pink wisp had just been dust. There was a strange smell in the air. Not unpleasant, but not quite like anything Myra had ever smelled before. It was like the outdoors at night, crossed with the overwhelming perfume shops at the shopping centre. She liked it. It smelled like excitement.

"Does your sister wear perfume?" asked Myra.

"What? Random? NO!" Rohan leaned down to pick Shilpa up from the cot, murmuring, "It's OK, the fire isn't coming here."

When his hand touched her arm, he gasped. "Her skin, it's sticky!" he shuddered.

"What? She's always sticky. She's a toddler," pointed out Myra.

Rohan didn't answer. He was trying to lift his sister out of her cot, but she seemed to slip away each time he made a grab for part of her body. Myra had never seen his eyes so wide and scared. This was no longer worry. This was terror.

Myra grasped at Shilpa herself, to help him, but the child felt wrong. Shilpa seemed to slide around under Myra's fingers, like jelly in a plastic bag. Horror flooded through her and, instinctively, Myra flung the child away. *Ew! Get it away! What is it?*

"MYRA!" Rohan yelled.

What have I done?

Myra's stomach dropped like a lift shaft. But as Shilpa hit the floor, she didn't cry. She sat up, with an expressionless look on her chubby little face. She was almost perfectly still. Rohan kneeled down beside her, reaching out to touch her.

Relief whooshed through Myra. *She's OK. I haven't hurt her.* She kneeled down beside him, leaning over Shilpa.

"I think she's OK," Rohan murmured. "But why did

you throw her like th— OH."

In that moment, Shilpa fell sideways and melted into the carpet.

All that was left were her pyjamas, few wisps of pink mist and a scattering of sparkling dust motes.

"NO!" yelled one of them, or possibly both of them. Time seemed to slow.

They kneeled in total silence for a moment. Myra felt as though she was a million miles away from her body, staring down at herself, looking small and bright on the carpet next to the spot where Shilpa had been just a moment before.

Now there was nothing there except Shilpa's empty Spider-Man pyjamas, looking like discarded laundry. She turned to look at Rohan. He was shaking, hand over his mouth. The utter despair on his face made her want to get up and run and run and never look back. *I threw her and then she melted.* She shook her head. *It wasn't my fault. Throwing babies doesn't make them melt.*

Does it?

Then that smell came back. The perfumed, outside smell. Myra realised they were not alone in the room. She grabbed Rohan's arm, almost drawing blood with her ragged nails.

"WHO IS THAT?" she squawked, pointing at a

bright-green woman who was now standing in the corner of Shilpa's nursery.

3

Meet
Mab

"Hello," said the woman. She was dressed in skin-tight gold trousers, purple spike-heeled boots, a bright-pink sparkly top and a yellow top hat. She also had bright-green skin, which was … interesting. Maybe Myra's mum wasn't the only one who thought facepaint made a good party.

The woman looked at Myra's wellingtons, which were almost exactly the same shade as her skin, and gestured to her own face. "That colour is so NOW."

"Thank you?" said Myra.

Where did she come from? She couldn't have come through the door. I would've seen.

The green woman was leaning on the fireplace beside the floor-length mirror as though she'd been hanging out there for hours.

"Did *you* bring her?" Rohan demanded.

"Never seen her before," swore Myra truthfully. She

wished she *had* seen the woman before. She looked AMAZING. "Who ARE you?"

"My names are many, for I am awesome. Some call me Maberina Hawthorn Duessa Spenser-Mead McSparklefist McGie. But you can call me Mab for now. Greetings!" The woman leaned forward and gave a dramatic bow. As she did so, Myra realised that out of the back of her sparkly pink top hung a pair of gossamer wings, like a dragonfly's, reaching all the way down her back to her bottom.

"OH MY GOD!" Myra screamed, as her brain made a KER-CHING sound of realisation. "You're a FAIRY!"

Myra half expected Rohan to say that wasn't possible; fairies aren't real. But he was standing still as stone on the spot where his sister disappeared. His face looked blank, like he wasn't taking any of this in.

Mab bowed. "Guilty," she said. "Since you know my name, what are yours?"

"I'm Myra and this is Rohan," said Myra. She felt a strong urge to curtsey. She wasn't even sure what a curtsey was, but it definitely sounded like a thing you should do around beautiful magical fairy women in sparkly outfits.

"Only one name each? Disappointing," said Mab. Her

29

green forehead dipped into a frown – without wrinkling, which was eerie. It was like watching a cartoon have facial expressions. Myra realised there was something not right about her eyes either. In the middle of her green irises, each pupil was a slit, like in a cat's eye.

"I've got more names," objected Myra. "But everyone calls me Myra."

"Well, isn't that tedious of them," tutted Mab. "Now, what do we have here?"

Faster than Myra's eyes could follow, Mab kneeled down and picked up Shilpa's Spider-Man pyjamas between finger and thumb. Her nails were long, purple and pointed at the tips, like claws.

"No, what are you doing?" gasped Rohan.

Mab shrugged. "Well, I can see why the queen didn't take her clothes too. Human clothes are so dreary," she said. She looked at Rohan and snorted, then turned to Myra. "I mean, yours might be OK if they weren't so…" She gestured at Myra's green wellingtons, tutu and bright, shouty T-shirt, "…matching."

"Hey!" said Myra. Her annoyance made her feel braver. Who was this fairy to come round telling her she was boring? "Tell this queen to give Shilpa back right now!" she said.

"Myra," said Rohan, in a quiet voice. He was still

staring down at the spot where his sister had melted. "She can't give her back. Shilpa's…"

He didn't say the word "dead," but it started to form on his lips.

Mab gave him a look like he'd said something incredibly stupid. "You think she's DEAD?" The fairy laughed. "Oh no. That thing that disappeared? That was just a copy. Fairies leave those behind to buy a little time, before humans notice their babies have been taken. They only last a few minutes before they melt, but it's usually long enough to get away. Your real sister is in Otherland. The realm where the fairies live."

Myra felt a huge sea-wave of relief. *I didn't kill her. This isn't my fault.*

She glanced at Rohan. His face was somewhere between horror and wonder. "She's … not dead?" he said, in a tiny voice.

Mab shook her head. As she did so, a haze of glittering light drifted around her. She seemed to carry a spotlight with her, wherever she moved, except the light came from everywhere and nowhere. She was beautiful. Myra felt like she could gaze at Mab forever. Just looking at her was like being at the best party in history. It was like listening to your favourite song for the first time. Except it wasn't yours and would never be yours.

Rohan seemed less impressed. His expression hardened. "You have to give her back!" He paused for a moment, then added, "I'm sorry. I mean… Please?"

Myra wanted to laugh. Only Rohan would feel guilty about not being polite to a kidnapper. She managed to keep it to a suppressed snort. Still, Rohan glared at her like she'd pooed on his bed and blamed the dog.

"I didn't take her," said Mab. She shrugged. "So I can't give her back."

Rohan gave her a puzzled look. "What are you doing here then?"

Mab grinned and looked directly at Rohan. "I am here to take you … drumroll, please…"

A drumroll started up out of thin air, making Myra and Rohan jump

"…to Otherland, to rescue your sister from the fairy queen," she said, waving both arms with a TA-DA flourish. "When a child is taken by fairies, only mortals can rescue it. I thought everyone knew that? So come on!"

Myra had a sudden worry. Rohan was going to go with this woman and she was going to be left behind to explain everything.

And, even worse, she was going to be left behind by this wonderful being and possibly never see her again.

"What about me?" she asked.

"Sure, this is definitely ALL ABOUT YOU," snapped Rohan.

That stung.

"Don't worry, I'm taking you both!" said Mab. "Baby-rescuing fun for all!"

Myra clapped her hands. *Everything is going to be OK. Correction. Everything is going to be awesome! I'm going to go with her to Otherland and I won't be left behind. Everything is definitely amazing and not terrifying!*

Rohan's face didn't agree about the amazing part. It was frowning. It was one giant gloomy boy frown, with added glowering eyebrows. Myra had never seen anyone whose eyebrows could hold so much emotion.

"I don't like this," said Rohan. "Why are you helping us? You're a fairy. Your queen stole my sister!"

Mab let out a peal of laughter. It sounded like heaven on a Saturday night.

"Yes, I'm a fairy … and that's exactly WHY I am helping you, silly boy!" she said. "Isn't it obvious? I'm your fairy godmother," she said, making her TA-DAAAA motion with even more drama than before.

"My fairy godmother?" said Rohan weakly.

"Technically, I'm fairy godmother to both of you," she said, nodding to Myra too. Myra beamed, feeling a warm fizz. She'd never had a human godmother, never mind a fairy one.

"Us godmothers are thin on the ground these days," Mab went on. "Good fairies, generally, are in short supply. More and more fairies are siding with the wicked queen Gloriana. Apparently being a good fairy just isn't in style any more." She sniffed. "Personally, I'm trying to bring it back. It's retro, you know, being good. Like puffy sleeves. Or lutes."

"I…" said Rohan. He blinked. "This is all very confusing."

Mab smiled. "Excellent. I'd worry about my fairy-like abilities if mortals understood me too well."

"Has anyone ever told you you're really weird?" asked Myra in an awed voice.

"So many people," grinned Mab. "But it's sweet of you to say so too."

"Are you sure my sister is OK?" asked Rohan.

"No, I'm not sure," said Mab. "But the quicker we get there, the better our chance of saving her."

"Then we need to leave. Now," said Rohan. The panic behind his eyes was rising.

"Woo! Let's go!" said Myra. She felt a ball of glowing, fizzing energy inside her. Something was going to HAPPEN. Something big. Her tiny life was about to explode into something else.

But what if…

She stuffed all the annoying fear down into a hidden place, where she put a lot of things she wasn't sure what to do with. It was where she put the night the police were called because her mum and dad were fighting. It was where she put the feeling that she was too much and not enough at the same time.

She took a deep breath.

"Otherland, here we come!" she said, with the brightest smile she could muster, and a feeling of being very far away from her own feet.

Mab gave her a clap on the back. "That's the spirit! There's someone who doesn't care if terrible things happen, as long as there's fun along the road! Let's go!"

"How do we get there? To Otherland?" asked Rohan. "I'm not allowed to take the bus on my own…" he added uncertainly.

"I don't know what a bus is. But we can steal one later if you like. For now, we're going through the door." Mab pointed at the mirror.

"That's a mirror," objected Rohan.

"Only if you look at it through the eyes of human habit," said Mab. Her eyes twinkled as she spoke. Literally. Flashy lights sparked in the green of her irises.

Myra felt if she looked too long, she could be sucked into those eyes, like an astronaut sucked out of an airlock into starry, empty space, with her chest crushed by the void, and she would spin and spin forever and ever and…

Mab was still talking. "If you look at it another way… Mirrors are thin places. Doorways to Otherland. Places where real and unreal swap round. It's how the fairy queen crept into your realm and took the child."

Rohan flinched at that, but Myra looked at the mirror in wonder. A magic mirror! "It's like something out of a fairy tale!"

"Oh, it's so much better than that. Fairy tales always leave out the truly incredible bits," said Mab. "Plus, the fairy godmothers in them are so boring. Using mighty magical powers to make dresses and get people boyfriends! It's insulting, frankly. Plus, in fairy tales, fairy godmothers sometimes don't even get invited to parties! No one has EVER not invited ME to a party, I can tell you. Except this one." She looked at Rohan and Myra. "That was very rude of you both, now I think about it."

"Sorry," said Rohan. "I didn't know I had a fairy godmother."

Myra let out an exasperated noise. She thought that Rohan would probably apologise for his face being in the way if you punched him.

She felt a cold hand in hers. Mab was suddenly standing between Rohan and Myra. Her grip was powerful and her nails were sharp.

"What are you doing?" asked Rohan. "Wow, you're strong."

"Ow, get off," Myra said, trying to wriggle out of Mab's grip. She couldn't, though. The hand was like a vice.

Doubt rose like a bubble inside her. *Is this a terrible, bad, dangerous idea?*

She pushed the fear down again, from chest to stomach, where it fizzed inside like indigestion. Like her mum said, there was never any point being scared. Bad things would happen whether you were scared or not, so you might as well not be.

"We have to be touching or you'll get lost," said Mab. "You really don't want that to happen. Not unless you fancy having a leg where your nose is, or living forever in a howling void of chaos?"

"Dunno, I quite like chaos…" mumbled Myra. "Not the nose thing, though."

Without warning, Mab leaped and pulled them into the air, almost yanking Myra's arm out of its socket, until a warm tide of tingly light surrounded them and her arm went slack. She, Mab and Rohan were floating mid-air in a cloud of light for a moment, then Mab's wings flapped for two brief, powerful strokes, launching them directly at the mirror.

The very solid, very made-of-glass mirror.

"NO!" Myra screamed, expecting her face to smash and rip on splintered mirror glass.

But instead, her face hit something soft and cold and thick, like diving into a swimming pool of oily yoghurt. She tried to scream, but nothing came out.

4

The
Meantime

They were in the middle of nowhere and the middle of nothing. Myra felt sticky tendrils sliming over her face and hands, pulling her in and onwards. It was like being trapped in cobwebs – cobwebs that dragged at you, attaching all over your skin, smothering you, creeping down your throat.

Can't breathe.

Myra tried to cry out again but the invisible cobwebs filled her mouth and nose.

This is bad, she thought.

Then she thought nothing.

Possibly forever.

Maybe just for a second.

She came to with a massive gasping breath that dragged painfully through her chest. She opened her eyes. A beach of black sand spread out and down to a glassy blue sea. Rohan was crouching a few feet away, panting for breath.

The sun was so hot that it felt like it was poisoning her brain. The light flashed painfully bright, like a nuclear bomb on the horizon, then faded into grey, but the temperature didn't drop.

"Phew," said Rohan. "Does your stomach feel like it's got a tumble dryer inside it?"

"My head's pounding," Myra groaned. "But now you mention stomachs, I'm starving. Where do you think we are?"

"Otherland?" suggested Rohan.

Myra wrinkled her nose. "I've always pictured fairies living somewhere sparkly and beautiful and full of flowers, not empty like this place."

"I've not spent much time picturing where fairies might live," said Rohan in a dignified voice. "But wait … where's Mab? She was just with us."

Myra couldn't see her anywhere. She felt the tiniest stab of worry that Mab had dropped them in the void on the way to Otherland and now they were stuck here.

The beach around them was as empty as a desert. Myra took a handful of the black sand and let it run through her fingers. "It feels so cool," she said. "It's nice."

"Weird," said Rohan, also picking up a handful of sand, as though he didn't trust her. "In this sun it should be scorching," he added. "But it's like it's been in the fridge."

"We are definitely NOT in the fridge," said Myra. In fact, sweat was starting to dribble down the back of her neck. She felt as though her brain might liquefy and dribble out of her ears any second.

"So hot…" Rohan gave a sudden gasp and turned to her, his worry glands pulsing. "Myra. What if we're in hell?"

Myra groaned. Why did Rohan's brain always go to the worst possible option? If you told him he'd won the lottery, he'd probably assume it was the lottery for who was going to get eaten after a plane crash in the mountains.

"Hell?" she said. "That's a bit extreme, isn't it? We're on a beach!"

"We just got teleported out of my house by a fairy after my sister melted into the ground," said Rohan, folding his arms in front of him. "So don't tell me what's extreme. I am reacting the right amount to the utterly crazy events of the past five minutes."

Myra was annoyed that he had a point, so she ignored it and decided to use logic – his own weapon – against him. "I don't think it is hell, though," she said. "There aren't any demons, and we're not being prodded by hot pokers."

"Yet," said Rohan, ominously.

41

Myra stood up, brushing the sand off her tutu, and took a few paces towards the sea. Rohan got up and joined her.

The two of them looked out over the water for a moment. It was perfectly flat, untroubled by waves.

Myra fixed her eyes on the distance, trying to make out land, or something other than the big blue empty horizon. The blankness of the landscape was starting to creep her out. Though she definitely wasn't scared. Her heart was just going a little quicker than usual with all the excitement. *This is an adventure. Adventures are exciting, not scary.*

Then, with a splash that made Myra almost leap out of her skin, Mab's head bobbed up from the sea and she spat a jet of water at them, drenching them completely.

A second later, they were perfectly dry.

"Did you miss me?" asked Mab.

"Yes!" said Myra. "I mean … we weren't scared. But it's easier to be excited when you're around."

"You got that right," said Mab, preening as she swam.

"Is this Otherland?" called Rohan.

"What? How dare you!" said Mab, swimming closer to them then standing up after a couple of strokes. The water only came up to her ankles. Myra blinked. Mab opened her hand and showed them a crab. It had wings. She released it, and it flew a few inches before disappearing in a mist.

"Nothing stays still here for long. Nothing has true shape. It's too slippery even for fairies," said Mab. She made a face. "I REALLY hate it here."

"Where are we?" asked Myra.

"This is the Meantime. Between times. Between worlds. Like sand between your toes." She splashed closer to them. "We'd better get going. My magic doesn't work here, and there are … things that live here too. We're in a lot of deadly danger. Isn't that fun?"

Myra tried to feel the fun. All she could find inside her was a sinking feeling. It was time to give herself a talking-to. *What would Mum say? You've been transported by magic to another realm, and all you're doing is feeling sorry for yourself? What a waste!* She slapped on a big smile and said, "YES! So much fun!" which made Mab grin.

"You're not a very good fairy godmother, bringing us here if it's full of deadly danger," said Rohan. "Shouldn't you be keeping us safe?"

"Safe? DUST, no. I'm here to make your life more *wonderful*," said Mab.

"It's not been feeling very wonderful since you arrived," said Rohan.

"I'm just getting started, my little rosebuds," said Mab.

She let out a whistle so loud that Myra wondered if her eardrums would ever be the same. She also wondered if Mab would be able to teach her to whistle like that.

A rushing sound filled the air. Myra looked up at the swirling sky. Against the strange light of the Meantime she saw two vast black shapes, each with wings the span of a small aeroplane.

"Transport," explained Mab, as two monstrous black birds landed with a thud.

They were the size of elephants, with feathers as dark and shining as an oil slick in moonlight. Myra thought they looked like ravens or crows, but their legs were yellow like a chicken's and their eyes shone like glitter balls, full of floating specks of sparkle. She felt like her brain was floating too, floating away into the creatures' eyes. She couldn't decide if she disliked the feeling, or if she liked it too much.

"What ARE they?" she asked.

"Are they some of the … bad things you said live here?" asked Rohan, taking a few steps away from the birds.

"Aw, they're not so bad," said Mab. "Like everything here, they're leftovers. Scraps of other things. Memories of other birds. And there's nothing bad about birds. Well. Most birds." She fluttered her wings into the air and gave one of the bird things a pat on the head, scruffling its head feathers. It cooed at her with the voice of a dove.

"You want us to ride on a bird made of memories? That doesn't sound safe," said Rohan.

Mab laughed at him. "Where's your sense of adventure?"

"I left it in my other jacket," said Rohan. "It's in the same pocket that I keep my desire to plummet horribly to my death."

"Ha!" said Mab. "I didn't know you were funny."

"Apparently being about to die brings out my inner comedian," said Rohan.

Mab offered a purple-nailed hand to each of the children. Then, without waiting for them to be ready, she yanked them all into the air, depositing each of them onto one of the birds. Then she settled down in front of Myra on the front creature. "BIRDS! TO OTHERLAND! CHILDREN! HOLD ON!"

The birds flapped their gigantic wings, whipping up a wind that woke the dust around them, and whooshed into the air. Myra felt her stomach drop out through her feet. The ground disappeared beneath her and she clutched at the bird's feathers. As it flew up and up and up, she let out a joyful shout. "This is the best!" she screamed over the wind.

Behind her, Rohan was screaming too.

"I'M GOING TO DIE, I'M GOING TO DIE!"

"He's less funny now," said Mab sadly. "Apparently it's only *medium* levels of fear that make him funny."

Myra looked back, feeling a bit guilty, though she wasn't sure why. It wasn't her fault that Rohan was scared. He should be enjoying this. They were FLYING!

Rohan had his eyes screwed shut.

"Open your eyes!" Myra yelled back at him. "The view's amazing!"

"I'd rather not see the ground plummeting towards me!" yelled back Rohan. "I don't want to see death coming. Death can just sneak up on me gently and put me out of my misery, thanks!"

"Suit yourself!" yelled Myra, and looked down at the view below. A vast sea stretched out. A sea full of what looked like … people?

"That's the Sea of Abandoned Dreams," said Mab.

"Are they drowning?" Myra yelled back over the whipping wind.

"No, they ARE the sea. The sea is made up of every abandoned dream and hope of humankind. Look! Someone must have wanted to be an astronaut. I think she's waving! Wave at the astronaut! Oh no, wait. She's not waving. She's flailing in misery."

Below was a sea of wriggling bodies in various costumes.

The things people wished they'd done with their lives. As they flew on, she saw a little bookshop with a striped awning, bobbing among the writhing figures.

Wait.

Was that her mother she saw down there?

A woman who looked very like her mother was certainly down there, dressed as a Hollywood star but holding a handful of balloons, walking along a very wet red carpet. No, it wasn't a carpet. It was a pile of red nappies. Myra blinked. It must have been her imagination.

"Are those real people?" Myra asked.

"No, they're just ideas. Things that could have been if life had been different," said Mab. "The real people are still in the mortal realm."

"Well, that's OK then ... I guess," said Myra. But she couldn't take her eyes off the misery below her, searching for another glimpse of the Hollywood star who looked a lot like her mother.

Mab pointed to the distance, beyond the sea of bodies, where a field of multicoloured flowers lay. Sunlight shafted down from the sky in beams so bright they almost looked solid, pointing the way. In the middle of the field, in the centre of the sunbeams, was a two-trunked tree with blue bark and bright-red leaves. "The way to Otherland!" cried Mab. "DOWN, BIRDS!"

They swooped, and the flowery field grew closer and closer. The bird carrying Myra and Mab levelled off and glided to the ground, landing with a gentle thump. Mab lifted Myra down to the ground with a gentle flutter of her wings.

Once safely on the grass, Myra turned to see Rohan's bird coming in to land. Rohan was screaming, "STOP! STOP!" but the bird was diving practically straight down.

The ground was only feet away now. The bird wasn't stopping.

"NO NO NO NO NO!" shrieked Rohan.

The bird's beak slammed straight into the ground, sending a shudder through Rohan that even Myra felt. The boy tumbled off the bird's back, bouncing down its wings and hitting the flower-strewn ground with a jarring bump.

Rohan groaned and staggered to his feet.

"Well, you didn't die!" said Myra brightly.

That only made Rohan groan louder.

The bird itself was sticking out of the ground by its beak like a spade someone had stuck into the earth. It didn't seem too bothered. It just blinked at them with its sparkling eye.

Rohan gestured back at the creature. "Why did you give me a broken one? I could've been killed!"

"It's not my fault you can't drive," countered Mab. "Why didn't you learn?"

"Because we don't have giant chicken ravens where I come from?" said Rohan, exasperated. "Giant chicken raven driving lessons are definitely NOT on the curriculum at school."

"That's sad for you," said Mab. "Come on." She offered an arm to Myra, who took it, and they skipped off towards the tree, giggling. The smell of the flowers rose up around them, new scents released each time their feet hit the ground, from sweet butterscotch to fresh-mown grass. Each time they skipped, the flowers sprang up behind them, like they were made of plastic.

"Wait for me!" said Rohan. "And of course you're immediately BFFs with the dangerous stranger," he called after Myra.

"You wish you were BFFs with her," Myra called back.

"And you're having fun when Shilpa's in danger!" Rohan added. His eyes were pleading.

That made Myra feel bad. Not bad enough to let go of Mab's arm, though. There was a buzzy hum to the touch of the fairy's skin that was both comforting and thrilling. They stopped by the two-trunked tree.

"How do we get through?" asked Myra. "Do we climb the tree?"

"No, but I like the way you think," said Mab. "For a human, you're almost imaginative."

"Almost? I'm *way* imaginative," said Myra.

Mab stuck out her forked tongue, then laughed. "Maybe a little. Now, here's how. Put your hand on that whorl." She indicated a swirly pattern of circles, one inside the other, on one of the tree's trunks. Myra put her hand in the middle.

"OH!" She half withdrew her hand. "It's sinking in."

"It's meant to," said Mab. "Go on!"

Myra put her hand more confidently on the tree this time, and it sank all the way to the elbow.

"Now push through."

"How do I...? Oh," said Myra. She smiled. The tree seemed to turn to water as she pushed. A way was opening. It was like the mirror door from her world to the Meantime, only much less sticky and gross. "Now I get it," she said.

She stepped forward and the darkness swallowed her.

5

Creative punishments

Myra was in a forest, standing on soft moss. But it was like no forest on Earth she'd ever seen. The scents were so powerful, they seemed to fill her lungs like liquid. She couldn't even begin to describe them. Her senses were flooded and all she could take in were snatches at first.

Everything around her glistened like it was wet.

Glowing from the inside. The moss at my feet, like cats' eyes on the motorway, glowing in reflected light.

The trees were in full leaf and covered in pink flowers. Those flowers had thorns and some were watching her with glowing eyes, from deep within the blooms.

"Wow," said Rohan, stepping out from a tree. On this side, the tree door was hundreds of feet high and bright, shocking pink. "I can't … I can't take it in."

Myra inhaled deeply. Things were starting to come into focus. The longer she stood, the less overwhelming it was. The more she felt…

This is somewhere I belong.

Mab stepped out through the tree, raising her hands in a "TA-DA" gesture. "Welcome to Otherland! I'll be your guide this evening. It's always evening here. Well, twilight. Do you like it?"

"It's beautiful!" breathed Myra.

"It's horrible," gasped Rohan. "I feel like my brain is going to pieces! Can't make sense of it all."

"You'll get used to it," said Mab. "Or you'll lose your mind. Either way, you'll stop going on about it."

Rohan just groaned. Myra felt a little thrill. There was finally something she was better at him at: being in Otherland.

She felt like she was coming to life. Every part of her was singing.

Through a break in the trees the sky above them was a blue-pink twilight; not light, not dark. There were no stars, no sun, just a luminous tinge to the swirling misty heavens above. At their feet was a cluster of pink and purple mushrooms, gently pulsing to a beat they couldn't hear.

That's when Myra saw something so adorable she wanted to squeal. It was a furry little creature with big brown eyes and floppy ears. The thing made a cheeping sound like a baby chick, so she obviously had to kneel down and stroke it immediately.

"It's so sweet!" she said. "What is it?"

"Oh that? That's Oberon," said Mab. "He used to be her Favourite ... I suppose mortals would call that a boyfriend or girlfriend ... but then he displeased the queen, so she turned him into ... well, not sure. But he is rather sweet."

"So ... does the queen turn fairies into other ... things ... often?" asked Rohan.

"All the time! Though sometimes she does worse things." Mab made a face. "Sometimes she banishes fairies to the Meantime."

"It wasn't so bad there," said Myra.

"For fairies, it's horrible to spend too long in the Meantime," said Mab. She gave a little shudder. "It's a non-place, where nothing ever really happens. Your magic doesn't work, which feels like losing a limb. Plus, there's no one really around to show off to! That's like being deprived of air or food for fairies."

"Do even good ones like showing off then?" asked Rohan.

"Hello, have you MET me?" laughed Mab.

The tinkling sound of her laugh made Myra feel happy to be alive.

"Just because I'm a good fairy, doesn't mean I have

to be a tedious fairy."

"But…" Rohan frowned. Apparently the laughter didn't work on him. "Showing off isn't something good people do!"

"Who says?" said Mab.

"My mum. My dad. My aunties," said Rohan. "My teachers."

"My mum says showing off is just your body's energy finding its way into the world," said Myra.

Rohan snorted in frustration. "This isn't getting us anywhere." He put on his best grown-up face, which was where he dialled up his worry so high it made him look twenty years older. "How are we going to rescue my sister?" he asked Mab.

Mab flashed them both a delighted smile. "Never fear! Your fairy godmother has a plan! You see, the queen – like all fairies – loves games. So the way to get a changeling back is through a Knight Game."

"Is that like chess?" asked Rohan.

"I don't know what chess is. Is it a quest made up of a series of trials of increasing difficulty, facing mortal perils, tricks, monsters and horrifying terror? Because if it is, then, yes, a Knight Game is just like chess," said Mab.

Rohan and Myra exchanged looks.

"Oh," said Rohan. "That's … not what chess is like."

Myra felt a flutter of excitement. Whatever lay ahead might be dangerous, and it might be terrifying… But oh! She felt alive. This was big. This wasn't what a little, squashed person did. Quests were for people who mattered.

"What are you looking so pleased about?" asked Rohan.

"Nothing," said Myra. "I just think … we can do this. We're going to win this game, whatever it is."

"And we'll have fun doing it," said Mab. "We haven't had a Knight Game around here for a hundred years. It's SO retro!"

"You think mortal peril and monsters are fun?" asked Rohan.

"When it's not me facing them, yes!" said Mab brightly.

Myra couldn't help laughing.

Rohan was not laughing. His mouth was set into a grim line. She couldn't tell if he was terrified or angry. Maybe both? Angrified?

"If we survive this Knight Game, what happens?" asked Rohan.

"You get your sister back," said Mab.

Rohan breathed a deep sigh of relief. "Oh," he said. "Good."

Mab raised a finger. "There is one catch. If you lose

the game, you'll have to stay in Otherland forever."

"That might not be so bad," said Myra. She looked around her at the glittering trees and inhaled the perfumed air. "I think I could like it here."

"This place," muttered Rohan. He shivered. "I can't think straight. My brain feels foggy, like I'm half asleep."

Myra frowned. She didn't feel asleep. She felt soothed. Like all her worries were just drifting away like balloons into the sky. Her mind was full of softness and warmth. Rohan just needed to relax. He might start enjoying himself.

Mab led them into an open space between the trees. Myra stared around in awe. It was the most wonderful place she had ever been. There were giant, shining silver flowers that reminded her of hubcaps, vines that undulated like pretty snakes, and eyes in the trees around the glade. Not in between the trees. *In* the trees – the bark of the trees around them were studded with glaring, staring eyeballs.

"Gross!" said Rohan, at exactly the same moment that Myra said, "Amazing!"

"Welcome to the glade of suspense!" said Mab, gesturing around.

"Why's it called that?" asked Rohan.

"Wait here and you'll find out," said Mab, disappearing

with a puff of pink smoke.

"What?" said Rohan. "Come back! What's going on? What's going to happen?"

Myra snorted. "Oh, I get it. The glade of suspense."

Rohan stomped his foot. "I can't believe her! This is no time for dad jokes!" Then his anger faded and the worry dialled up again. "I wish my actual dad was here. He'd know what to do."

"Relax. Look around you. It's amazing," said Myra. She wandered over to inspect one of the silver flowers. As she drew close, it made a purring noise.

"I can't relax. The trees are staring at us," said Rohan. He folded his arms. He looked ridiculous here in his stiff shirt and tie.

"They can't help it," said Myra, giving the eyes a little wave. "They don't have eyelids. Or necks. So they can't turn and look away." She breathed in deeply, smelling the flowers. The scent made her feel a deep sense of calm, as though nothing could ever go wrong again. She reached out to touch one of them.

"Don't!" called Rohan. "Don't touch anything!"

Myra wasn't having that. There weren't even any signs saying don't touch. Mab never told them not to touch anything. So it was definitely allowed. Myra stroked the petal of one of the shining flowers. As she did so, the petals turned into a shower of silver raindrops, floating upwards. As they drifted over her head, Myra saw a rainbow in the water beads.

As they faded, she turned to look at Rohan. "See. Touching it turned it into something even more brilliant!"

"Yeah, but the next thing you touch could bite your hand off or something," said Rohan grouchily. *That boy does NOT like to be wrong,* thought Myra. "Anything could happen here!" he added.

"You say that like it's a bad thing!" said Myra. Being here, she felt as though this huge weight was lifted. She could really breathe. There was no one lurking around a corner to tell her off. No one knocking on the door to take stuff away because her mum hadn't finished paying for it. And she didn't feel too much or too loud here. She didn't feel squashed and small. She felt just right.

Mab appeared in a puff of rainbow smoke and sparkles.

"Did you enjoy your suspense?" asked Mab.

"Myra touched a flower and it turned into a rainbow," said Rohan, snitch that he was.

Mab turned to face Myra, looking very serious all of a sudden. "Did you?"

Myra swallowed. *I spoke too soon. Someone IS going to tell me off.*

"Then I have something to tell you," said Mab. Her

catlike eyes bored into Myra's. Myra felt sweat prickle at her hairline and in her palms.

Then Mab burst into a grin. "I like you," she said. "Touching things without worrying that they might be dangerous? That's cool. That's smooth. You could do well here."

Myra let out her held breath and waggled her thick eyebrows at Rohan, as though to say, "See! It WAS fine!"

"This time," said Rohan.

"Now," said Mab. "The fairy queen will be ready for you in mere moments."

"Where are we going?" asked Rohan.

"Nowhere," said Mab. "She's coming to us."

6

The throne
that moves

The mossy ground near them was moving, like a travelator at an airport. Myra had only been to one airport, when her dad left to live in Spain. This travelator was much better. It wasn't carrying someone away. It was bringing someone closer.

And what a someone.

A wonderful throne was gliding towards them. Fairies of every shape and size flew around it in a cloud, so Myra couldn't make out the figure sitting on it at first. Some of the creatures were small and furry. Others looked almost like insects, with bug eyes and antennae. Others still had antlers like stags and manes like lions.

"Some advice," said Mab. "Be polite. The queen is easily insulted. Call her 'Your Gracious Majesty' a lot and generally bow and scrape."

"I think I want to be sick," whispered Rohan.

"I'm not an expert on manners," said Myra. "But I'm

guessing that's not the best way to introduce yourself to an easily insulted, magical overlord from another dimension."

"Depends on her mood," said Mab. "She might find it funny. As long as you aren't sick on her."

"I'll aim for Myra," said Rohan. But then he was quiet. They all were. The queen was here.

The throne stopped a few feet away from them. The cloud of fluttering fairies parted and drifted to the ground, revealing the queen in all her glory.

And it was a LOT of glory.

She was the most beautiful thing Myra had ever seen. She sat on a throne made of what seemed to be bones and winding gold weeds, vibrating with magic.

"Unicorn bones," whispered Mab. "You can tell by the way they glow."

The queen's shimmering face was as many colours as Myra could imagine – and many more she couldn't. Her hair was piled on her head in ringlets that defied gravity. Looking more closely, Myra saw that a flock of butterflies was holding it up by the ends.

Gazing at the queen, her eyeballs seemed to quiver. She rubbed them, but it didn't help.

"You'll get used to it in a few minutes," said Mab.

Myra wasn't sure she'd ever get used to any of this, not

if she lived to a million years old. She wanted to put her thoughts into words, but all she could say was, "Mum would KILL for that dress."

"All rise for the Great and Glorious, the Bringer of Light and Noise, the Very Beautiful, Very Clever and Very Wonderful Queen Gloriana!" announced a fairy the size of a mouse. It was green and bald and flew on bat wings over the queen's head. Its voice was loud and low, quite out of kilter with its size.

"Approach, mortals!" cried the queen.

Myra felt the moss beneath her feet moving, pulling her helplessly closer to the queen. She let out a little "Wheee!" as they went.

"You're loving this, aren't you?" Rohan hissed.

"May as well enjoy the ride," said Myra.

"I bet sometimes you're having a nightmare and you stop halfway and think, THIS IS BRILLIANT, don't you?"

"You really hate fun, don't you? What did fun ever do to you?"

"It blew up my shed! And last year it put my party magician in hospital!"

But their bickering was stopped by the sudden halt of the moss, which sent them sprawling at the fairy queen's dainty purple-webbed feet. Myra noticed that she wore a shimmering ring on each of her webbed toes.

"Leave us!" The queen's voice rang out and she pointed a long, long arm at Mab. "Good fairies are permitted to exist because I am gracious. But I don't want to have to look at your unfortunate face for longer than I have to! You're as hideous and disgusting as a grogworm from the Pit. You're ORDINARY."

Mab held up her hands in surrender. "You are as fair and just as you are beautiful, my queen," she said. "I AM a grogworm, in comparison to your magnificence. I will take myself away."

She turned to the children. "But if you need me, call for Mab and I'll come running. Or flying. Or … well, I may come by carriage, if I'm in a carriage sort of mood. Or I might ride a giant beetle. Giant beetles are very in right now."

"I notice that you are still here," said the fairy queen in a dangerously quiet voice. "Against my express wishes, you continue in my presence. It would be a terrible shame if I accidentally turned you into something as a result."

"Noted," said Mab, and she vanished in a puff of apologetic smoke.

Myra felt a lurch of panic.

They were alone with the wicked fairy queen, in Otherland. And she didn't look pleased.

"Now. What do you want here, human children?" asked Gloriana.

Myra couldn't take her eyes off the woman. She'd seen beautiful things before in her life. Her mother's gold-spiked platform shoes, for example. But nothing like this. It was like gazing at the most beautiful sunset, but if that sunset was also an exploding star, and that exploding star was riding a unicorn. With wings.

Myra's palms were sweating. She was sure there was something she was supposed to say, but her mind was a complete blank, apart from the fizzing whizzing feelings in her eyeballs. *Why are we here again? Where am I? Who am I?*

"Oh, Gracious Majesty," said Rohan. His voice wavered with nerves but his eyes were bright and full of purpose. "Please, would you give my sister back? Mab said if we took part in a Knight Game, we could win her back. So I would like to … do one of those."

Apparently, Rohan wasn't having the same trouble holding together his train of thought in the presence of the queen. He'd clearly got over his brain fog.

The one thing I was better at than him – being in Otherland … and now he's caught up and taken over, thought Myra.

The queen raised a perfect green eyebrow. Then she threw her head back and laughed. It sounded like tinkling bells, if tinkling bells wished very bad things to happen to you.

Then the queen looked right at them. It sent a shiver through every cell of Myra's body.

"I accept your challenge," she said. "Did you hear that, my people? A KNIGHT GAME! A CHALLENGE! These tiny mortals will face three terrifying, twisted tasks of my devising. If they succeed, they will win my changeling back for the mortal realms. If they fail, they will stay here forever."

She looked Rohan and Myra up and down. "Although, perhaps not in those particular, tedious shapes."

The fairies roared with applause, squeaking and wailing and howling with delight. The clapping grew louder and louder, and the squeals and wails grew darker. Myra had a sudden feeling of doubt. A tiny voice deep inside whispered, *I want to go home.*

"You can go home if you like," said the queen – possibly reading her mind, though perhaps reading her face instead, which was a mask of horror. "I can send you back there with no child and your tails between your legs," said the queen. "I'm happy to add the tails, since you lack them at present."

"No!" said Myra, with a defensive grab at her bottom.

"Then let the games begin!" said the queen.

"Wait," said Rohan. "Before we start, I want to see my sister first. To see she's OK. Please?"

"Oh, she's BETTER than OK." The queen grinned. Her teeth glowed a fluorescent yellow and, Myra noticed with fascination that they appeared to be filed to points. Was that a hint of a snake tongue flicking between them, too?

The fairy queen made a sweeping gesture and a gigantic purple flower grew up from the ground, filling the air with… Myra couldn't describe the smell in terms of things she'd ever smelled on Earth. It smelled like the feeling of someone pinching you hard on the arm. It smelled like the feeling of being about to cry. It was a cruel smell that woke you up screaming in the middle of the night and at the same time made you wish that you could sleep forever.

With a snap of the queen's fingers, the flower's petals peeled back and inside sat a small figure, dressed all in green.

It was Shilpa.

Rohan rushed towards her. "Shilpa!" He reached down to touch her, hugging her tight, then pulling away as she didn't respond. "You're OK! Aren't you?" he said. Then he looked into her eyes.

Myra could tell from Rohan's horrified face that the

little girl wasn't OK. Myra looked closer and saw that Shilpa's eyes were no longer a pure dark brown. They were flecked with bright green, like splinters of emerald glass had been crunched up inside her irises. Myra took a step closer. The smell … it was coming from Shilpa. Tears pricked her eyes and her stomach tightened.

Rohan turned to the fairy queen. For once, he didn't look timid. He looked angry. "What did you do to her?" he blurted. Then, a moment later, added, "Your glorious majesty."

"It's not 'glorious majesty' any more," said the feathery-scaly fairy. "That's so over. Address her as Lady of All Light and Fire, if you please."

"Lady of all light and fire…" began Rohan.

"You didn't say the capitals," said the feathery-scaly fairy crossly.

"…what's happening to my sister?" finished Rohan, ignoring the correction.

"You're going to LOVE this," said the queen. "I'm turning your sister into my changeling. Which is halfway to a fairy. And before long she'll become a full fairy. One of us. Not one of you." She wrinkled her nose. "Lucky for her!"

Rohan went pale.

"But … why are you doing it?" asked Myra.

The queen glared at her. The feathery-scaly fairy poked Myra in the arm with a very sharp claw.

"What?" said Myra.

"Use the title," hissed Rohan.

"Oh, right. I mean, why are you doing it … Your Glorious Majesty, Lady of All Light and Puppies?" she added.

"Close enough," said the queen. "Well, since you are clearly very ignorant humans, let me explain to you the facts of life. Unlike crude fleshy humans, we don't grow small people inside ourselves."

She made a face. "A disgusting idea." She shuddered all over. "Instead, we fairies make more fairies by stealing humans and turning them into one of us. Born out of theft, all fairies start out in life with a kernel of trickery and naughtiness. Isn't it great?"

"OW!" Rohan let out a blistering yell.

Myra saw him clutching his hand, while Rohan's little sister stood grinning up at him with sharp teeth that she hadn't had an hour before, and blood around her mouth.

"She bit me! Bad Shilpa!" he said, sucking his finger.

Shilpa continued grinning, like an evil doll.

"Oh, you lovely, naughty little changeling," said the queen. She patted Shilpa on her curly head. Then she extended her arms to the children. "And just think… if you lose the Knight Game, you too could go through this glorious change!"

"No thanks," said Rohan. "And … Shilpa will turn back to normal, if we win, right?" He was watching the fairy queen closely.

"More or less," sniffed the fairy queen. "Probably."

"Probably?" Rohan almost choked on the word.

"If we turn into fairies, will we be all tall like you?" said Myra, gazing up at the beautiful queen. Myra had always wanted to be tall. Her mum was tall. It made you look more dramatic.

The queen laughed. "Oh, sweetie, you'll be nothing like me. You'll be my servant. However, you might become an interesting fairy, perhaps," she conceded. "You do have something about you." She looked deep into Myra's eyes.

Myra met her gaze, fascinated, almost hypnotised.

Rohan nudged her. "Turning into fairies and becoming her servants is the BAD thing, remember. That's what happens if we *lose*."

"Yeah, yeah, I know," said Myra. But she still gazed at the fairy queen, feeling wistful. There was something about being here that made her feel truly free. There was an energy, a fizz to everything.

The queen stretched up her arms and gave an enormous smile. "I'm excited about this, I won't lie to you. Now, ready or not … let the Knight Game begin!"

7

The Wild Wood

The fairy queen clapped her hands and her throne began to revolve, taking the children and the patch of glittering moss where they were standing along with it. When they stopped, they were facing a tangled wall of trees, with a small, dark opening leading underneath the branches and through into the forest.

"Welcome to the Wild Wood," said the queen. "Your first task is to enter the wood and find something I lost. A jewelled scarab beetle necklace that a human gave me once. Well, *gave* is a strong word. And did I mention that the human was dead at the time? OK, I stole it from a pharaoh's tomb. But what's important is that it's mine, it's lost, and I want it."

"Why can't you go and find it yourself?" asked Rohan.

"Don't be ridiculous." The queen's beautiful face took on a look of pure scorn. "You can't go after your own lost things, it doesn't work that way. And none of my fairies are brave enough to go for me. Cowards, the lot of them, bless their pretty little yellow hearts. They're more ornamental than they are bold. So I'm sending you."

"So we just have to find a lost necklace? That sounds pretty easy," said Myra.

"What's the catch?" asked Rohan. "What are the fairies scared of?"

"Oh, no catch. What makes you think there's a catch?" said the queen. "All you need to do is reach the Lost Cave, beyond the Wild Wood, find the scarab, and bring it back to me. There's just one small rule to follow: don't stray off the path while you're in the Wild Wood."

"Why?" asked Myra.

The queen glanced over to the forest, then down to inspect her nails, which seemed to have grown since last time Myra had looked. They were now rainbow-coloured, too. "Well, the full name of the place is actually *The Wild Dark Scary Creepy Wood of Death and Face-Eating Monsters Where Nobody Goes Unless they Really, Really Have to and Even Then They Prefer Not To*," said the queen. "If that gives you a hint? The path is protected. The rest of the wood is not. That's why fairies are scared of the place. Sticking to the rules – following the path – isn't in their natures, so rather a lot of them get eaten. Which is very inconvenient, given the poor supply of changelings these days. In any case, I recommend you stick to the path," she sniffed. "If you like your faces, which ..." She looked them up and down. "I'm not sure why you would."

"Hey!" said Myra. "My face is brilliant. You're the one with the stupid face."

"Careful! I've smited mortals for less!" said the fairy queen. She drew herself up and began to glimmer in a threatening manner. "Or is it smote? Smitten? Who cares!"

Rohan was hopping from foot to foot. "Shall we go? I'm not saying I'm super keen to risk getting my face eaten but ... can we start?"

The queen raised an eyebrow. "Eager, aren't you? Well. Jonny Squarefoot will guide you to the edge of the Wild Wood," she said, gesturing to a creature that stood on two legs like a human, but had a pig's head, and trotters for hands. Then the queen, and all her fairies, disappeared with a flash of light that seared Myra's eyes, and a smell of broken promises.

"She definitely knows how to make an exit," breathed Myra. Now that the queen was gone, she felt a little empty.

Jonny oinked at them and motioned to follow him. She looked him up and down.

"He's got a pig's head," said Myra. "That's cool. I wonder if fairies come with all kinds of animal heads?

73

Or if she turned him into a half-pig as a punishment?"

"Please, Myra, don't get distracted while we're in that wood. We have to stick to the path or die, remember?" said Rohan.

"I can be distracted and walk at the same time," said Myra, giving him a scornful look. "It's called multitasking."

Rohan just made a face, and they followed Jonny Squarefoot, carefully watching their feet so as to stick to the pale chalky path edged with pink moss. It wound ahead of them between glowing trees.

"Is this the Wild Wood yet? It's not very creepy," said Myra as they walked.

Jonny Squarefoot didn't answer. Myra hated it when people didn't reply to her. It made her feel like she was invisible.

"Excuse me," she said. "Mr Jonny."

The pig-headed man stopped and turned. He oinked as though to say, "Yes?

"What are you?" asked Myra.

"That's a really rude question," hissed Rohan. "You can't ask that!"

Jonny Squarefoot oinked in agreement, then turned and carried on down the path.

"It doesn't matter if we're rude. This isn't a manners test," said Myra.

"No, but if we're rude to him, he might lead us off the path in the Wild Wood and we'll get our faces eaten," said Rohan.

The trees around them were laden with fruit of every colour, including some colours Myra thought she'd never seen before. Some of the fruits looked like pineapples, but instead of spiny leaves, they had feathers. Others looked like mangoes, but smelled like chocolate.

With a grunt, the pig gestured that they had reached their destination. "The Wild Wood begins here," he said, in a low, snuffly voice. "This is as far as I'll go."

"So you CAN talk!" said Myra.

Jonny Squarefoot ignored her. "Jump down the back of the sofa," he grunted. "That's the way to the Lost Cave."

Then he turned and trotted off back down the path to the fairy queen's throne glade.

"But…" Rohan called after him, but he'd already disappeared into the shadows. "What sofa?"

But Jonny didn't turn back.

"Great, good job being rude to him," said Rohan.

"I wasn't rude, I just wanted to know whether he was half-pig, half-fairy, or if some fairies naturally have pigs' heads," said Myra.

Rohan shook his head. "Never mind. Let's go. Don't forget to stay on the path."

The edges of the path they were walking on were now marked out with gemstones that glowed, although the path itself was plain old chalky, dusty earth. The trees around them were thick and lush, with huge drooping leaves and gigantic colourful flowers in their branches. Shafts of sunlight pierced the canopy of trees from time to time, and the light seemed almost to dance across the forest floor, lighting up the tree roots and glistening on deep, calm pools and babbling streams. For a wood apparently filled with horror and danger, it was actually pretty special, Myra thought.

A sudden moan from some hidden creature emerged from the depths of the undergrowth. It made it slightly harder for Myra to appreciate the beauty of her surroundings. It's hard to look around and think, "Ah, lovely nature," when nature's looking back at you thinking, "Ah, lovely dinner."

Myra and Rohan walked in single file, both eager to keep to the path after the queen's warning.

Another babble of animal noise surrounded them, erupting into growls and roars from time to time, although no creatures were visible.

"I wonder which of those are the creatures that eat faces?" Myra wondered out loud.

"Just … look at your feet."

"Fine," grumbled Myra, and concentrated on putting one foot in front of another. It wasn't that hard. The path was wide enough. She didn't see why there was any harm in just making conversation.

The path continued winding back and forth and around in what felt like circles.

Eventually, they rounded a corner and the path opened out into a looser stretch of woodland. In the middle of the path was a battered old sofa. It was one of the least magical things Myra had ever seen. It was the sort of sofa people left out in the courtyard of her estate.

"There it is! The sofa Jonny Squarefoot told us about!" said Myra.

"But what do we do now? He said to go down the back of it. What does that mean? Get behind the cushions?" Rohan inspected the sofa, pulling the cushions away from the back to see what might be down there.

"Here, get back, I'm going to try something." Myra took a few steps back to get a run-up, then jumped feet first over the sofa.

"MYRA! NO!" came Rohan's voice from very far away.

For a moment, she was in darkness. Then she was standing on the path again. She turned round to see that the sofa was gone and behind her was nothing but mist.

Or was it fog? Myra never knew the difference. Cloudy grey stuff, anyway. The fog-mist rose up in a straight line, like a wall from the ground to the sky, all the way behind them.

With a thump, Rohan landed behind her. "Phew, that worked," he said. "You just disappeared and I thought…" He shuddered. "But then I figured whatever happened when we went through the mirror and the tree, this must be something similar. Some kind of portal. I wonder how they work."

"Who cares?" said Myra. Magic didn't need an explanation. That was the point. It was magic! "Now, where's the Lost Cave?"

To either side of them was what looked like a blank desert of mud and stones. Ahead was a sloping hill covered in green moss, with trees on one side. At the bottom of the treeless side of the hill was a dark cave mouth.

"That must be it!" said Rohan.

When they entered the cave, it took a while for their eyes to adjust. Myra glanced back and realised that the cave mouth was no longer there. Neither was the cave.

8

The Lost Cave

Instead of a cave roof, there was a starry sky above them, twinkling through a canopy of trees. And instead of rocky cave walls, trees stretched as far as Myra could see.

Hanging from the branches of the nearby trees were what looked like thick clumps of multicoloured fruit.

Only, they weren't fruit, Myra realised as they got closer. One of the clumps of "fruit" was a remote-controlled toy car. Another was a patterned scarf. One tree branch was draped all over with damp socks.

"Can I help you?" came a deep male voice.

Myra and Rohan looked in the voice's direction and saw a big burly white man, with a deep reddish tan, coming towards them through the heavy-laden trees. He was wearing a scruffy leather jacket and jeans. He had thick stubble, lots of curly black hair twined with the odd strand of grey and a round, friendly face with only a hint of wrinkles at the eyes.

Myra instantly liked him. He looked like Santa's younger brother.

"'Ello," he said.

Myra and Rohan stood up a little straighter. Something about the man screamed **Authority**.

"Hi," they said in unison.

"Sir," added Rohan.

"Suck-up," hissed Myra.

"Hi. I'm Tony Toestepsson," he said, brushing something off his hands. "Hmm. Oil. Must be from that abandoned car washed up this morning. Excuse me if I don't shake your hands."

He held up his big, rough palms for inspection. They were, indeed, smeared with black oil.

"Hi," said Rohan. "I'm Rohan Patel and this is Myra Duffy. We're here on a, er, quest. I realise that sounds a bit weird when I say it out loud."

"I've heard weirder," said Tony. "Nice to meet you, Rohan and Myra. Welcome to the Lost Cave."

"Oh good, we're in the right place," said Myra.

Rohan was gazing around at the trees with an intense expression.

"Penny for your thoughts?" asked Tony.

"Are all those things in the trees things that people have lost?"

Tony nodded, stroking his scratchy chin. "Aye. Bright boy. This is the Lost Cave, and those are the lost things."

"Why are they in the trees?" asked Myra. "Do they grow on there?"

"Nah. They're just there to dry," said Tony. "See, all the lost stuff washes up on the shores of my kingdom from the Sea of Oblivion, which stretches between the Meantime and everywhere else. I fish stuff out of the sea, dry it off, and look after it until it's time for it to be returned to its owner."

He reached up and plucked a sock from the tree, giving it a rub to check if it was dry. "This thing, though, it's fated to stay here forever. It's one of the permanently lost things. Socks so often are."

Myra had to agree. She hadn't worn a pair of matching socks since she could walk. Though perhaps that was less about socks and more about her mother, who thought that matching pairs were for people with no imagination.

"Are there a lot of things that are lost forever?" asked Rohan.

"Things ... even people," said Tony. "There's a whole lost city called Atlantis in a lake out the back. I go and visit the king there sometimes to watch the footie."

Lost forever. Myra sometimes felt like that herself. Like a balloon floating loose, with no one holding the string.

"Could the thing we're looking for be permanently lost?" Rohan asked. His worry dial was clearly starting to click upwards.

"Well, we'll have to see, won't we?" said Tony, pulling a cloth out of his jacket pocket and getting some of the oil off his hands. He spat into the cloth and rubbed his hands again. "If you're meant to find it, you'll find it. Though," he hesitated, "you're not looking for something *you* lost, are you?"

"No, we're looking for a scarab necklace belonging to the fairy queen," said Rohan.

"Phew," said Tony. He jerked his head forward, indicating that they should start walking. "That's the one rule of this place – you can't find anything you've lost yourself."

"Why's that?" said Myra, striding as fast as she could to keep up with Tony.

"Maybe everyone would come here then?" suggested Rohan.

"Quite right. I'd never get a moment's peace," said Tony. "People would come here all the time. Well, not fairies, what with them being cowards."

"So you're not a fairy?" Myra asked. "What are you then?"

"Stop asking people that," hissed Rohan.

"What? It's not like he's ashamed of what he is. Are you, Tony?"

Tony did blush a little. Then he said, "No, I'm not ashamed of what I am. I suppose you might call me a god?" He shrugged. "Depends on your point of view."

Myra's heart leaped. A god? Well, maybe there was *something* about him. A smell that wasn't quite human. A kind of fizzy lightning scent, half sweet, half bitter. It smelled at once comforting and terrifying.

"Not being rude but your aftershave is REALLY strong," she said, to distract herself from the terror.

Tony laughed. "I've been told that. But it's not aftershave. It's just me. We can smell a bit overpowering to humans, apparently. Sorry. Though it has the advantage of keeping the vampires away."

"Vampires?" said Rohan. "We're not going to meet any of them, are we?"

"Not here you won't," said Tony. "Vampires don't often get lost. Nor lose things. They're very meticulous, are vampires. Tidy."

"Do they sparkle?" asked Myra.

"Not unless you spill glitter on them," said Tony.

The trees around them were now bare of lost objects. Ahead was a large pair of metal doors, painted sky blue, embedded in a wooded hill. He pushed and they opened slowly.

"Now, here's where you might just find the thing you're looking for."

9

How do you lose a painting?

They were standing in the entrance to a vast warehouse, full of … stuff. There was no apparent order to the jumbled heaps of objects. A wooden horse on wheels was piled on top of a beach towel, in whose folds nestled a half-empty bag of sweets. Piles of coins, mostly pennies, were heaped everywhere, like the treasure trove of a dragon. In between the mounds of lost things threaded a system of paths, making it possible to access all parts of the room.

"Whoa," breathed Myra. "It's like the TARDIS!"

"It's even bigger than the TARDIS!" said Rohan.

"Actually, I think there are some lost episodes of *Doctor Who* around here somewhere," said Tony, peering towards a far corner of the vast space.

"This is just the first chamber," he went on. "There's obviously the stuff outside, but that was all lost in the past day, and none of it's a scarab necklace. So if the thing's meant to be found, it'll be in here. If it's meant to be permanently lost... Well, we can come to that if need be."

Myra was gazing around the room, realising what a large – and possibly impossible – job they had ahead of them. Better get going.

"I'll start over here." She ambled over to the nearest pile of objects and began picking up and throwing them over her shoulder when she was sure they weren't a pendant.

"Oi! Stop that!" growled Tony. "I've just sorted those!"

She stopped that. "Sorry," she said.

"Wow. You made Myra stop messing about and apologise? You really are a god," said Rohan.

Myra gave a snort and looked around at the random piles of stuff.

"You said you've just sorted this stuff but..." she said, "none of this stuff looks very sorted."

Tony laughed a deep laugh from down in his belly. "I know where everything is. That's all that matters. And when things are ready to be found, they turn up wherever they're meant to be."

"So if we're meant to find it, we'll find it?" asked Rohan.

"You're getting the hang of this," said Tony.

Rohan kneeled by a pile of walking sticks, umbrellas, toys and socks, carefully looking at each object then replacing it. Myra went to another pile and started going through that with theatrical over-caution.

Tony watched them, rubbing his chin thoughtfully. "What I want to know is why two human children are here looking for lost fairy possessions."

"The fairy queen's taken my sister," said Rohan, looking up from his search for a minute. "So if we find her this necklace, and do some ... other stuff ... she'll give my sister back."

"I see," said Tony. He frowned. "Sorry to hear about your sister. That's rough."

"Also, if we don't succeed, we have to turn into fairies and stay in Otherland forever," said Myra. "Which I'm *pretty* sure is a bad thing. Probably."

"All a matter of perspective, I suppose," said Tony. "For example, if I were your parents, I might be annoyed at that. And you've only just started your human lives, so it would be a shame to quit them so soon." He shook his head. "Honestly. Fairies. Nothing but trouble. Mind, they'd take that as a compliment."

"Do you think the queen knows if the necklace is a permanently lost thing?" Rohan asked Tony. "Like, has she sent us on an impossible mission?"

Tony shrugged. "I couldn't even start to guess what goes on in Her Majesty's head. It's like a nest of angry bees on a sugar rush in there. I take it this is one of those Knight Games that you're engaged in?"

Rohan nodded. "Yes it—"

"Is this a scarab?" Myra called, interrupting him and holding up a large metal necklace with a spider hanging in the middle.

"Too many legs!" Rohan called back. "We're looking for six legs. A scarab is an insect. Insects have six legs!"

"Spiders don't!" Myra called back.

"Spiders aren't insects!"

"But *this* is a spider," she said. "And it's clearly an insect!" She waggled the spider at him.

"Now I think you're just trying to make me angry!" Rohan yelled back.

He wasn't entirely wrong.

She grinned. "Stop interrupting me," she said. "I'm trying to search for the necklace!"

Tony was laughing behind his enormous hand. "Well, I'd better be off. I imagine a new batch of lost things will've washed up by now. If you want anything, just holler."

He gave them a sunny smile, then walked away whistling. Myra got up from her pile and wandered over to Rohan. She was starting to get bored just staying in the same place and wanted to explore.

"Tony said the thing will be found if it's ready to be found, right?" she said. "So I may as well wander around looking for it. It might jump out at me."

"Well, don't get lost yourself while you're looking for it!" said Rohan.

"Yes, Dad," scowled Myra, and wandered off.

She glanced at various piles of shoes, clothes and – in one corner – a sunburned man in a bright shirt. He didn't seem to see her. He was just wandering around, looking at a map. A moment later, he vanished.

Lost tourist? she wondered. As she went on, something shiny caught her eye. She kneeled down to see that it was a dagger in a shiny sheath. *Maybe that will come in handy later, if we have to fight anyone. Or anyTHING.* She tucked it into her pocket. There was a slight doubt at the very back of her mind. Was this stealing? Or was this just finding something that was ready to be found? *It's definitely the second thing.*

"Myra?" came Rohan's voice.

She stood up hurriedly and turned to him, making sure the dagger was fully in her pocket. Luckily, her skirt had deep pockets.

"Look, I think splitting up was a bad idea. I just saw a

strange man. I think we should stick together from now on," he said. He pointed to a door at the end of the room. "Shall we try through there?"

"Might as well," shrugged Myra, feeling the dagger slap guiltily against her thigh.

The door led to another warehouse of equal size. The walls of this room were decorated with old paintings.

"How much do you reckon that's worth?" asked Myra.

He shrugged. "Also, how do you lose a painting? It's not like you'd take it with you on the bus and leave it in a cafe."

Myra stopped suddenly. Something had caught her eye.

"Rohan! That's the scarab." She pointed upwards at one of the paintings lining the walls. There was a large portrait of a queen wearing a necklace with a jewelled scarab embedded in the centre.

"That's just a painting," said Rohan.

"Yeah, but it's the scarab we're looking for," said Myra. "I've just … got a feeling."

Rohan looked sceptical, so she poked her finger in the direction of the painting with a greater firmness. "Look at it properly. There's something … real about it, I swear."

Rohan stepped closer to the painting, looking at the painted scarab necklace with its large red gemstone and glorious feathers.

"The stone … it looks like it's moving," he breathed. "Even though the painting isn't moving. It can't be."

Without knowing quite why, Myra reached up – and into – the painting. Her arm disappeared up to the armpit. It felt like warm, tickly water, and she wanted to laugh. She felt her fingers close over something, and she pulled her arm back. When it emerged from the painting, she was clutching some beads. But there was more to come. She yanked and a second later she was holding a necklace, with a jewelled scarab beetle in the middle.

Rohan looked on, stunned. "That. Was. So. Cool," he said.

Myra was staring at the necklace in her hand. It was unreal. "I didn't expect that to actually WORK. Usually when I try something new, it blows up in my face."

"Literally," said Rohan.

"But that WORKED!" said Myra. She felt utterly baffled and delighted, and waved the scarab necklace at Rohan.

"Well done," said Rohan. Although he didn't look completely thrilled. "You're really acing this quest. Well, we'd better get back to the queen with the necklace."

"We should say bye to Tony first," said Myra. "Weren't you saying we have to use our manners earlier? Or is that just on fairies?"

"We should probably use manners on everyone," said Rohan.

Myra made a face and slipped the necklace over her head. It seemed to hum against her chest. "Tony!" she called.

Tony appeared in a puff of petrol-tinged smoke. "Everything all right? Oh, you found it already? Where was it?" He gestured to the necklace.

"It was in the painting," said Rohan.

"And you put your hand in it?" Tony raised his eyebrows and let out a low whistle.

"No, I did," said Myra.

Tony was looking at the painting and shaking his hand. "It's a good thing you didn't put your hand in the one next to it. That one's carnivorous."

He led them back through the warehouse, clicked his fingers, and they were in the garage in the wood inside the hill.

"Here," said the god, pulling a couple of paper bags out from his pockets. "I brought these to you. Shouldn't go to Otherland on an empty stomach."

The children looked inside, and the bags were full of food. Not just any food.

"My favourite!" said Myra, pulling out a peanut butter

and jam sandwich and biting into it. She peered into Rohan's bag. He had a dosa.

"Still warm!" said Rohan. He took a bite. "Mmmmm!"

Myra saw there was another one in the bag. She pinched it, taking a big bite. It was perfect. Just the right mix of crispy and spicy and stodgy.

"Hey! That's mine, put it back," said Rohan.

Myra opened her mouth to show the chewed-up dosa. "Oo ant it ack?"

"Ew, no," said Rohan, snatching the unchewed part back but gesturing for her to shut her mouth.

She smiled and swallowed gleefully.

"How did you know dosa's my favourite food?" asked Rohan.

"And how'd you know peanut butter's mine?" asked Myra.

"Like I said, I'm a god," said Tony. "Some gods know everything. I just happen to be good at finding things, and guessing what people's favourite foods are. Now, come on."

Tony led them back out of the garden, along the lost river, through the garage and out on to the road. "Just hop back over the sofa and you'll be in the Wild Wood," said Tony.

"Thanks, Tony," said Rohan.

"Good luck!" said Tony. He snapped his fingers and the sofa appeared on the road ahead of them, as moth-eaten and lumpy as ever. "There you go," he said. "Just jump over it from the back to the front."

"Thanks!" said Myra.

"Ready?" asked Rohan.

She nodded. They turned and jumped out from behind the sofa.

10
Myra's liver

They were back on the path in the Wild Wood, clutching bags of food, surrounded by glowing lights and growling sounds. Myra tried to shove her sandwich bag into her pocket so she could have her hands free, and as she bent over to shove it down, the dagger fell out of her other pocket.

"What's that?" asked Rohan.

"My dagger," said Myra. She picked it up and showed him the jewelled hilt, not quite able to look him in the eye. "I found it in the Lost Cave," she said.

"You STOLE it?" Rohan stopped and stared at her. "You have to take that back! Tony was so nice to us and you STOLE from him?"

She was shaking her head. "No, see, I worked it out. It's not stealing. Tony said if something was supposed to be found, then you'd find it. So I found this dagger ... which means it must be me who was meant to find it."

She gave him a bright and breezy grin that was brighter and breezier than she felt.

"Myra! Have you never read any Ancient Greek myths? Don't you know what happens when you STEAL THINGS FROM GODS?"

"No," she said. "I like Norse myths. They're weirder and have more giants. What happens when you steal from Greek gods?"

"You get your liver pecked out for all eternity," said Rohan tartly.

"Well, Tony isn't Ancient Greek, he's called Tony," said Myra. "And I'm sure he wouldn't mind."

That was a fat lie. She definitely wasn't sure. But she hoped he wouldn't.

"Well, anyway," she went on. "We don't know what the next trial will be, do we? Maybe we'll have to fight something and we'll need to be armed."

"You should take it BACK, Myra," said Rohan. "You don't know what Tony might do when he finds out!" His eyes were sparkling with anger now. Myra didn't like that sparkle at all.

"Don't you get it," spat Rohan. "You can't just *do* things like you would at home. Things have consequences here – real ones. Not just getting excluded from school or going to jail. We could be killed!"

"No, YOU don't get it," Myra shot back, sticking the dagger back in her pocket. "The rules are different here. If you can make them work for you, it doesn't matter if it's not the 'right' thing to do," she said. "This isn't like home. There aren't any parents or teachers or police. It's ... sort of like a game. You shouldn't be able to put your hands in paintings, but I did, and I can! Everything's different here!"

Rohan snorted so hard a little snot came out. "This is ridiculous. Fine. Let's go and take the scarab back to the queen, but if Tony comes after us, I'm telling him it was you."

"Fine, that's just fine, it WAS me. But if some monster needs stabbing later, you're not borrowing my dagger," said Myra. "And you can't have any of my sandwiches either!"

They were stomping along, not looking each other in the face.

"How do you manage to ruin EVERYTHING?" raged Rohan. "Quests, birthday parties..."

"I brought those fireworks to make UP for ruining the party last year!" Myra yelled back. "I thought you'd like it! I was trying to be nice!"

"You thought I'd like you setting the garden on fire, did you?" Rohan brushed a frond out of the way, purposefully pinging it back in Myra's face.

"OW!" Myra batted the frond out of the way, rubbing her cheek. "How was I supposed to know the shed would catch fire just from a few fireworks? I can't see the future!"

Rohan was staring straight ahead, stomping onwards down the path. He was yelling now. "I can definitely see a future where, if we ever get home alive, I don't want to see your stupid reckless face ever AGAIN!"

"Fine by me!" Myra shouted back. "I know you hate me anyway so why would I want to be friends with someone who—"

"MYRA!" Rohan yelled. "STOP!"

Myra froze.

"Look at your feet," he said.

She did so. "Oh," she said, in the quietest voice she'd ever used.

In her fury, she'd stepped across the gemstones that bordered the path.

Into the Wild Wood.

Her feet seemed suddenly very far away.

"Get back on the path," Rohan hissed.

Myra stepped back over the stones, carefully, slowly. There was silence in the forest for a moment. None of the animal noises they'd heard before. No monster noises, either...

"Maybe it's OK?" said Myra. Her heart was smashing against her ribs like a really stupid fly trying to get through a closed window. "I only stepped off for a moment."

A deep, throaty laugh emerged from the foliage around them. Or maybe several things were laughing. The cruel cackling echoed all around them.

"That is not a good sound," said Rohan. "That is a sound I do not like."

"Come on, let's just keep going," said Myra. "I'm back on the path now; nothing can get us."

Idiot, croaked a voice.

Imbecile, shrieked another.

Fool, howled a third. *You've left the path once, so you're ours now, wherever you stand in the Wild Wood!*

There was a great thrashing and a roaring, and the sound of branches breaking and leaves shaking. Something was approaching the path. Some*things*.

"Run!" Myra shoved Rohan forward, breaking his petrified trance.

They ran, Rohan just behind Myra.

"Take that!" she shrieked, throwing the sandwiches back at the creature, then running again. There was a chomping sound.

Nice of the snacks to bring snacks, came the horrible voice.

The thumping footsteps of the unseen creatures were

on the path now. Screeching sounds filled the air, and the crushing-crashing footsteps of enormous creatures. It was impossible to tell how many of them there were. Myra couldn't stop herself from glancing over her shoulder.

The glimpse gave her a jumbled impression. Monsters, for sure. One hairy creature with a long pink scraggy neck. No eyes in its face, just teeth. Another with a squat, scaly body, and six legs. Another looked like a huge snake with insect legs, its fangs gleaming.

The things were getting closer, snapping at her. *Faster*, Myra willed herself. *RUN FASTER*. Her wellies slapped against the ground. When she'd got dressed this morning, running from monsters had not been part of her fashion considerations. She could hear the beats of Rohan's feet hitting the ground as he ran behind her.

Myra's lungs felt like they were bursting open from the pressure. But she ran on, legs pumping, not looking back again, feeling terror in every inch of her – a terrible fear of stumbling and being grabbed up into one of those mouths. And then, in an instant, her fear came true.

Only not for her.

There was a scream. She looked back. Rohan was being pulled up into the air by the snake-like creature. He was screaming at the top of his lungs, beating the thing with his fists, kicking his legs, but it made no difference.

"Help! Please! No!"

Myra stopped dead, totally helpless. She had nothing to fight the creatures with. Her dagger? Way too small to do more than annoy the monster. It'd be like fighting a lion with a needle. The creature was easily a hundred feet tall!

This wasn't like in Thronehammer, when she could just rush in with a reckless attack and be brought back to life by Rohan on the next turn. If she rushed in now, she'd be dead, and there'd be no resurrection spell.

The snake creature was holding Rohan by his collar. He looked so small.

Myra felt helpless.

"ROHAN!" she yelled, but didn't move.

The things weren't just mindless monsters; they were full of malice, enjoying the fear. The hairy creature snapped at Myra, close enough for her to smell its foetid breath. It grinned an eyeless smile of victory.

It spoke in a voice like death itself. *Come here, child, this can be over quickly.*

"I don't know what to do!" screamed Myra, looking up hopelessly at Rohan, whose face was contorted in fear. "I'm sorry! I don't know what to do!"

"HELP!" Rohan screamed at the top of his lungs. He struggled, wriggling free for just a moment, dropping a few feet, but another monster caught him in its sharp claws, biting into the flesh of his shoulders through his shirt and making him yell louder.

"HELP!" screamed Myra. "Someone!"

A thought blossomed in her mind. She had one last hope. It was a very thin, flimsy hope, but it was the only hope available.

"MAB!" screamed Myra. "HELP US!"

Then several things seemed to happen at once.

Something whipped past Myra, knocking her to the ground with a WHOOSH of air.

There was another WHOOSH and Rohan was lying on the ground beside her, looking bloody and dazed, but alive.

A great howl went up. Then a bang and a cloud of glittering smoke puffed out through the trees. There was a crack and a squeal and yet another howl. And another. And a hiss, and a snap, and a familiar voice screeching, "LAY OFF MY HUMANS! EAT DUST!"

Then a bang, and several great rustling thumps of very large bodies falling in a wood, another puff of glittering smoke, and Mab was standing beside them. She was wearing a bright-red skintight outfit, like a superhero, only with a cloak made of gossamer. Her hair was piled high on her head, like some kind of eighteenth-century painting. She spread out her arms in a TA-DA gesture. "How many fairy godmother points do I get out of ten? How much do you worship me right now?"

Rohan, lying bloody on the ground, gave a moan.

"Eleven points, you say? Eternal gratitude and worship, was that?" said Mab, putting her hand behind her ear and leaning closer to him. "Why, thank you. I think that was some truly extraordinary fairy-godmothering, if I do say so myself. Frocks for a ball are easy. Beating up the faceless face-eaters is next level!" She gave a bow.

"You saved us," said Myra, staggering to her feet. "That was incredible! How did you do it?"

"See, *she* gets it," said Mab. "And I used fairy dust, of course! The source of all the best battle magic." She patted a bag at her belt and indicated the glittery stuff on her palms.

Myra reached out to touch it, then licked her glittery finger. It was gross.

She wrinkled her nose. "Bitter!"

"I should think so," said Mab. "Considering where it comes from."

"Where DOES it come from?" asked Myra.

"Well, let's just say, nectar and ambrosia go in one end," said Mab, pointing to her mouth. "And fairy dust comes out…"

Myra felt like she might do a bit of sick. "Oh."

Rohan stifled a snort of laughter.

"Don't laugh," said Myra. "You've got it all over you as well."

Rohan wiped his hands and face hurriedly on a nearby leaf.

Mab peered more closely at Rohan. "Oh dear. Are those wounds fatal? I've not seen a human bleeding close up before."

"It's just a scratch," said Rohan, looking at the puncture marks in his shirt and wincing a little.

Myra had a thought. "Hey, those creatures weren't poisonous, were they?" she said. "Cos if they were their poison might be in Rohan's blood now and—"

"What?" said Rohan. His face was pale beneath the streaks of blood.

"Oh no, they're not poisonous," said Mab. "Plenty of poisonous creatures out here in the Wild Wood. But those particular ones are just razor-sharp of teeth and claw. You were seconds from certain death. But I saved you, and you're all right!" she said, beaming. "That's good, isn't it?"

"I'm in favour of not being dead, yes," said Rohan.

"For once, I agree with him," said Myra.

"Good, good, good!" said Mab. But then she frowned.

"I have to say, I feel … very strange. I should just feel glory and triumph at my victory. Instead I feel…" She cocked her head on one side and inspected Myra, placing a hand on her own chest. "In here, it's like there's a little trapped bird."

"Are you … scared? Have you never been scared before?" asked Rohan.

"I'm not scared," said Mab, thoughtfully. "I've been scared before. I mean, I could tell you stories of life during the Vampire Wars that would put your drab little human hairs on end, but this isn't fear." She clutched at her sparkly top, above her heart, looking puzzled. "It's like fear. But I don't feel it about me." She pointed at Rohan with her claw-like fingernail. "I feel it about YOU!" She pointed at Myra. "And you! So it can't be fear."

Rohan blinked. "Er … yes it can. You can feel afraid FOR someone else. It's called empathy."

Mab shook her head. "How dare you? Only humans feel that. Are you calling me a HUMAN?" She wrinkled her little green nose, looking very offended.

"There's nothing wrong with being human!" objected Myra. "Being a human is cool. We invent stuff. And we have TV. Do fairies have TV?"

"I don't know what TV is," said Mab. "Is it a food?"

"Wow. Otherland is properly backwards," said Myra

pityingly. "I bet you don't even have the Internet either!"

"Why would we need nets?" said Mab. "We don't eat fish. We eat nectar and ambrosia. And I'm feeling very attacked right now so I think we should change the subject to something that makes me feel good."

Myra frowned. "You're definitely not like the fairy godmothers in stories."

"That's because the stories were told by humans who'd probably never even met a fairy," said Mab. "Never mind a fairy godmother."

"Well, as our fairy godmother, do you have any tips for our next trial, before we go back to the queen?" Rohan asked.

"Tips? Tips. Hmm… Don't die," she suggested.

"More specific tips," said Rohan. "Such as … practical ways to avoid dying?"

Mab thought harder. "Well. I don't know exactly what the next trial will involve – it's different every time – but I do know that mortals can get very confused during the games. So try to remember that not everything is as it seems."

"I'm making detailed notes over here about that not at all vague instruction," said Rohan dryly.

"She's trying to help!" said Myra.

"Exactly," said Mab. She pointed to Myra. "Now. You

have the scarab, I see?"

Myra had forgotten about the necklace. She clasped it in her fist. "Yup."

"Then let's go and see the queen," said Mab, giving a little clap. "Well done, my unfairy godhumans! You've passed the first test!"

11
Halfway to fairyhood

The fairy queen Gloriana received them in her throne glade with all the warmth of an arctic winter in an ice age on a particularly snowy day.

"Ah. The fairy godmother and her mortal hangers-on." She curled her perfect green lip in disgust, then held out a sharp-nailed hand, palm up. "Give me the scarab," she added.

Myra shuffled forward nervously, holding out the necklace. Rohan was watching the queen closely, as though she might leap forward and eat them.

She probably wouldn't do that. Would she?

The queen snatched the offering from Myra's hand and popped the scarab out, throwing the rest of the necklace away into the bushes. The bushes rustled, and there was a crunching sound. Myra decided not to think too much about that. She also decided not to go too close to those bushes.

The queen licked the scarab. "Hmm … this appears to be the real thing." She peered at Myra. "Did you cheat?"

"No!" said Myra. "I just reached into a painting and pulled it out." She didn't mention that she had also helped herself to a shiny dagger. Long experience with adults had taught her that you should never share more information than they ask for. It only ever led to detention.

Gloriana turned her gaze on Rohan. "You're very quiet. I don't like quiet people. They're usually plotting something."

"Rohan's never plotting anything," said Myra. "He's a good boy."

Rohan gave her a fierce look. "A good boy? Do you know how patronising that sounds?"

"Oh, only about as patronising as you sound every time you talk to me," said Myra.

"Great, yes, let's definitely fight, that didn't nearly lead to me getting EATEN last time!"

Myra felt a stomach lurch at that. "That wasn't my fault!"

"You were the one that went off the path!"

"Only because you were being so annoying!" Myra shot back.

"Wanna see annoying? You should look in the mirror!" yelled Rohan.

A peal of tinkly laughter, like glass smashing on diamonds, filled the glade, louder than laughter should be. It was the queen. "Discord! Oh sweet discord! Children, you bring me great joy! I'd forgotten how much petty hate mortals carry with them. I should invite more of them here!"

"You didn't invite us here. You stole my sister so we had to come," said Rohan.

"Some invitations are written on paper. Others are sent using more creative methods," said Gloriana. She reached behind her throne and pulled something into her lap.

Someone.

Or ... no, maybe *something* was right.

It was Shilpa. Only not the Shilpa that Myra had known since she was a tiny baby. The plump, brown child with the shining black eyes was gone. Her eyes were completely green, shining with an eerie light.

All dressed in fluorescent green and yellow, this new Shilpa sat like a doll on the queen's lap. Her skin was greenish and her once-fat cheeks were sunken. Only her black curls were the same. She was laughing, but not in the cooing burble Myra was used to. It sounded ... cruel.

Rohan gasped. "Oh!" His voice was like a sad shadow.

"Isn't she pretty?" said the queen. "She's almost

halfway to fairyhood now."

"Stop it! Don't do this to my sister!" Rohan rushed forward a couple of steps but Myra came after him and grabbed him.

"Stop right there," she hissed. "Don't do anything stupid. That's *my* job."

The queen smiled unpleasantly. Her eyes had become large like saucers, yellow with the merest black dot of a pupil. "Listen to the girl. She knows me, I can tell. She knows what I am capable of. Because she is like me."

"You what?" said Myra.

"I can smell the chaos in your blood. It smells sweet," said the queen.

Myra gulped. "You shouldn't go round smelling people. It's rude," she said. But a tiny part of her was thrilled. *Am I really like her? Do other people see magic in me?*

The fairy queen ignored her and struck a pose, one slender hand on her hip, the other resting on her beautiful throat. Her expression was almost kind. She bent over the children wafting a mist of perfume all around them. Her face was so close to Myra's that it was disconcerting. She smelled like a hothouse of flowers. Myra's brain began to buzz. *Bees*, she thought. *This is what bees must feel like near flowers.*

"Now, never let it be said that I am not gracious in

defeat. To congratulate you on your victory," purred the queen, "I'm going to give you two gifts. The first is the gift of truth."

"What do you mean?" asked Myra.

"I wasn't talking to you," said the queen. She turned her gaze to Rohan. He looked down to his feet, unwilling or unable to meet her eye.

"The first gift is for you, little boy. I want to tell you the truth about how you came to be here in Otherland."

12

The gift
of truth

She waved at the children and conjured them a pair of chairs, woven from gold and blossoms. The chairs scuttled forward on little legs, forcing the children to sit by knocking their knees out from under them.

"Now, as you know," said the queen, "I came to you through a portal that you call a mirror. What you might not know is that such portals are rare these days. Our worlds have moved further apart since humankind developed irritating things like science and computers, so it takes a special event for a portal to open. The special event in this case was you two briefly dying as babies, on midsummer night."

"How do you know about that?" interrupted Rohan.

"Because I felt it happen," said the queen. "Or rather, it wasn't your death I felt … it was your return. That shouldn't have happened. Birth, death, and rebirth on the same day? It's too much back-and-forth between your realm and elsewhere. It tore a little hole in between the worlds with its wrongness. Both of you shouldn't be alive. You're mistakes." She gave them both a beautiful, terrible smile. "But the universe's mistake meant that, as soon as you were old enough, an enterprising fairy would be able to creep through the hole you made." She gestured to herself, in case they were in any doubt which enterprising fairy she was talking about. "It was only a very little hole, when you were babies. But it grew, until you reached the first magical age, at which point a portal opened. A portal that would open until sunset on your birthday." The queen paused dramatically.

"Oh!" said Rohan. "Is eleven the first magical age? And that's why you came through on our eleventh birthday?"

"Don't be a slug-brained pit fiend," scoffed the queen. "*Seven* is the first magical age. Everyone knows that, and it was on your seventh birthday that the first portal opened. That's when I was planning on slipping through to take any mortal babies or children I could find in the area near the portal. Now, it wasn't easy to pick the right moment. Mortal time moves more slowly than it does here, so keeping track of your sluggish human years took many complicated spells. But, because I am mighty and wonderful, I found a way. I had a spell all set to trigger when you turned seven. I was ready to come and snatch you the moment the portal opened – and any of your little friends who might be around."

"Then why didn't you?" asked Myra.

The queen sighed. "Stealing children is hard when there are adult humans around. Their love and protection repels my magic." She scowled. "It's pesky. I came close, mind you. When Myra's dad turned up and the odd ladies and gentlemen in tedious uniform appeared with flashing lights, there was almost enough of a distraction, but not quite."

"How do you know about that?" asked Myra. Her seventh birthday was something she tried not to think about. The time her mum and dad got into such a screaming row that the neighbours called the police.

"I've been watching," said the queen. "Not all the time – your lives are so tedious and your parties so depressing that I couldn't bear to spy for more than a minute at a time. But I wanted to know what I was getting myself into. I could have sent a servant, of course, but where's the fun in that? So I had to know if any danger lurked. Such as … iron weapons," she added with a shiver. "But luckily your houses seemed to be free of weaponry or guards."

Myra wasn't listening any more. She was thinking about something the queen had said. Gloriana had said that this was a gift of truth, especially for Rohan. Why, though? Why wasn't it for her too?

"I don't get why this is all about Rohan," she said. "You've been talking about stuff that happened to both of us. Our deaths tearing a hole ... our joint seventh birthday."

The queen gave her an approving look. "Bless you for trying to make this all about you; it's very fairylike. But the truth in question IS just for Rohan. The whole story might be about the two of you, but this little nugget of truth I have is a special gift just for him."

"Go on," said Rohan impatiently. "What's this truth you want to give me?"

"As I said, I tried and failed to snatch you and yours before," said the queen. "So, for my very special gift to you I want you to know that the reason I succeeded this time was Myra. It was all Myra."

The queen paused and looked, drinking in the expression of horror on Rohan's face. Myra felt a creeping horror all of her very own.

"I came through the portal on the eleventh hour of your eleventh birthday. But I still needed a distraction, to snatch me a changeling. When Myra set fire to that shed, she sent your parents running to the end of the garden, away from the baby. So unlike your seventh birthday,

116

when your parents hovered around the vulnerable children like eagles around their nests, this time I was able to slip in easily and take a baby. It was barely even a challenge. Honestly, Myra, you made it too easy. I feel I should almost be angry with you."

Myra felt her stomach drop. This *was* her fault. This was all her fault.

"Well," said Rohan. His lips were as thin as pencil lines and his eyes were bright black with fury. "That all makes perfect sense. Of COURSE this is your fault. Of course it is. Why am I not surprised? Because this makes PERFECT sense. Nothing has made more sense in the history of EVER!"

The queen looked delighted. "Oh, I'm so glad you like your first present! Look how much fun it's causing! Look how the boy is bristling!" Her eyes were eager. Perhaps she hoped Rohan would physically fight Myra. He looked like he wanted to.

But instead he just turned away. "I think I can do without the second present if it's anything like the first one."

"Oh, it's nothing like the first one," said the queen. "It's a delicious surprise."

The queen clapped her hands and a tall, elegant yellow fairy with floor-length white hair and tiny lizard-like eyes appeared with a tray.

She held it out to Myra and Rohan, glancing sideways at the queen. "Nectar? Ambrosia? Rose-petal consommé?"

"What do you fancy?" Gloriana asked them, indicating the array of delicate saucers and plates, all made from woven petals. They weren't on the tray, but floated inches above it. "I assure you, each one of these delicacies is more delicious than anything you've ever eaten before. If you don't taste it now, you may spend the rest of your life wondering what it might have been like."

"Ooh, I'll have two of each!" said Myra, reaching out and taking a couple of tiny saucers. The smell was amazing. She felt that one taste could take every bad thing very far away.

The look on Rohan's face when he discovered all this was her fault, for example.

Rohan slapped the petal cups out of her hands. "You're not supposed to eat fairy food! Did you even pay attention at ALL when we were playing Thronehammer? No, of course you didn't," said Rohan, aghast. "What if it's poison? What if it means you have to stay here forever?"

Myra looked at the floor. The scent of honey and ginger and spices drifted drowsily up through the air. She looked longingly at the spilled food. *Does the five-second rule apply in Otherland?*

"Or, fine, drink it and get stuck here forever," said Rohan. "Like I care. I'll finish the quest on my own!"

Without looking back, he stalked off.

"His loss," said Gloriana huffily. She waved at her servant. "Buttercup, these children don't want my second present. Take it away."

"No, wait," said Myra. She stopped the fairy carrying the tray. "Just because Rohan doesn't want it, doesn't mean I don't." She snatched a golden buttercup-cup full of some kind of clear liquid, and gazed into it. She wanted to show Rohan he wasn't in charge of her. She could make her own decisions. Why should he get to be Captain Rohan, supreme boss of all?

Plus, the stuff in her little cup smelled so good. Warm and spicy, sweet without being sickly.

So what if it DOES mean I stay here forever? Would that be so bad? Is the human world really all that great? And who's going to miss me? Not Rohan. Probably not my mum. She glanced at the queen, who was gazing at her with something that looked almost like love. *At least someone wants me around.*

There didn't seem to be a moment when she first took a sip. But as she drank, she forgot everything except the taste. It was sweet and warm and soft on her tongue. It ran down her throat like a rainbow. She was filled with light and joy.

Moments later, she was lost. Lost in lights and fire and the mesmerising stomp of feet and the pump of music. Raw, angry music, that thrummed and throbbed. Around her, a party was starting, and she realised she was dancing. It was like her body was no longer under her control – she was just one part of the whirling mass of fairy limbs and torsos, shimmying shoulders and swaying hips.

And it was wonderful.

13

The cave

Myra felt groggy. She blinked, to check she actually had her eyes open. She blinked a few more times and saw something very faint. Was that a glimmer of light in the distance?

She tried to move towards the light but her body felt heavy. She realised she was lying face down on a rocky surface. Her limbs felt awkward. Had she hurt herself? She couldn't entirely remember. The last thing she could remember was drinking that delicious nectar.

She found she couldn't stand up. Her legs were wobbly and just felt … wrong. So she crawled.

She glanced up as her eyes adjusted to the dark and saw that the ceiling wasn't far above her. She was in some kind of narrow tunnel. Good thing she didn't have claustrophobia.

It was always good to look on the bright side, she thought, even when you woke up in a dark tunnel and your legs didn't work. Her mum would be proud of her positive attitude!

If I ever see her again…

That's not very positive, is it, Myra?

Myra started to crawl towards the glimmer of light, which she hoped was the way out.

As she crawled, the light grew stronger. It began to hurt her eyes, until she found herself emerging from the darkness into blinding sunshine. A cool breeze blew fresh air into her nostrils. Not the perfumed air of the fairy glade, but a salty, clean breeze. It smelled amazing, like the most delicious meal she'd ever had. Speaking of meals, she could murder breakfast. She sniffed again. It wasn't just the fresh air that smelled delicious – she could smell food! And it was nearby!

Her eyes slowly got used to the light. It was morning – sun shone down on a green hillside covered in moss and tiny flowers, where white horses were grazing a few hundred feet away from her down the slope. No, they weren't horses. They had horns on their heads. Unicorns. *COOL!*

It was then she heard a clanking sound. Someone was coming. She saw a figure emerge from between the trees. A figure wearing armour, carrying a sword. A man? Or was it a fairy?

No, it wasn't a man, or a fairy. It was a small boy.

He tipped his visor back and stared at Myra with black, worried eyes.

"Well, this is it," said Rohan. He hefted his sword in both hands, holding it out carefully in front of him, as though scared he'd cut himself. Why did he look so small? Had he shrunk in the night? Perhaps the fairies had cast a spell on him? She had to help him!

"ROHAN!" cried Myra. Or she tried to. Something was wrong with her throat and she could only let out a grumbling groan. She must have lost her voice after all the shouting at Rohan last night.

Rohan flinched slightly, but then muttered something to himself and began to walk towards her. He began to raise his sword. His arms were trembling.

"Rohan, what's happening?" she tried to shout, but her voice failed her again. Was she ill? Her throat felt hot and dry and scratchy.

"Come on then, dragon!" yelled Rohan.

Myra looked behind her in terror. A dragon? Was it coming for her? But there was nothing behind her. And Rohan wasn't looking behind her. He was looking at her. Why did he look so small?

And now he was charging at her, yelling at the top of his lungs, legs pumping, sword arm waving all over the place. He ran faster than someone in armour should be able to run. Faster than she'd ever seen Rohan run. He swung the sword blade at her in an arc.

The blade bit into her arm and she tried to scream, but her voice emerged as a dry rumble. Her arm hurt, but not as much as you'd expect a sword slice to hurt. It felt more like a bad graze. She flinched.

Rohan swung back the sword. What was he doing? Why did he want to hurt her?

Then she realised what must have happened. He'd drunk the nectar! After telling her not to! Somehow it hadn't affected her, except to make her sleepy and heavy and hoarse. But it had sent him into berserker mode! He didn't even recognise her! Plus it had shrunk him!

She had to snap him out of it. She waved at Rohan frantically, screaming his name, or trying to. If only she could scream properly. If only she could break through his addled haze. He kept coming. She staggered back, stumbling awkwardly. She realised she was on all fours. Why did her body feel so strange? It was like she had new parts to her.

As Rohan approached again, she felt a burning sensation in her lungs and a strong urge to cough. As she did so, fire spurted out of the air, near her face. She ducked. Maybe there WAS a dragon behind her, but it was invisible?

Rohan roared in anger – or maybe in terror – and swung the sword at her again.

She managed to stagger back out of the way just in time. She let out a hissing breath of relief and the fire appeared again.

Deep, deep in her brain, the dots began to join. Fire. Rohan attacking. Talking about dragons.

Rohan wasn't attacking her. He was attacking a dragon.

And I'm the dragon, said a little voice. For once she didn't squish it down.

It was the nectar. It turned me into a dragon.

She tried to say, "Rohan, it's me! It's a trick!" but her words came out in a roar of fire.

So she put her hands to each side of her face and screamed in despair as he swung his sword towards her.

14

The humanity plague

The blade stopped inches from her face. Rohan dropped it with a clatter on the rocky ground and stared at her.

"Myra?" he gasped.

As he said the word, she felt her body shift. Her muscles moved beneath her scaly flesh and she was shrinking. It hurt, as though something was squashing her from every direction. She felt something dissolving inside her. All of her seemed to fade as she shrank. But then she felt something solid form within her. She was taking a new, smaller shape.

Her own shape.

Finally, it was over. She was crouched on the floor in last night's clothes, and bleeding. She looked up at Rohan, who was staring down at her with tears in his eyes.

Rohan reached out to help her up. "Oh, God, I'm so sorry, Myra. I'm so sorry!"

"How ... *cough* ... did you know it was me?" she

whispered. "Before I turned back?"

"Your scream," said Rohan. "I'd know it anywhere. I'm so sorry. Your shoulder, it's bleeding. I'm sorry."

Myra touched it tentatively, feeling a bit faint as the wound gave under her fingers. "Ew," she said, touching it again. She never could leave scabs alone.

"You were a dragon!" said Rohan in awe. "I'm sorry it took me so long to realise it was you."

Myra shrugged. She felt warm inside. He HAD recognised her. He hadn't just seen a monster. He'd seen her, through all the scales and fire.

Speaking of scales and fire… "Did I look awesome as a dragon? I bet I looked awesome."

"You looked so terrifying I wanted to wet my armour," said Rohan.

"I'll take that as a yes," said Myra. Then she looked at Rohan, remembering she'd been breathing fire. "I didn't burn you, did I?"

Rohan shook his head. "Magic armour. The queen gave me magic armour and a magic sword to protect me and make me super strong and fast. It seemed a bit suspicious at the time, why she was making my life easy for the challenge. But then I saw you, this massive dragon, and still wasn't sure that the magic weapons would be enough. You were REALLY big."

"Ah, when I first saw you, I just thought you were really small!"

"I'm five foot five!" objected Rohan. "I mean, including my hair…"

"Yeah but from a dragon's-eye view, that's tiny," said Myra. "I wish you'd taken a picture of me!"

"I was a bit busy fighting for my life against a monster," said Rohan. "Also, I don't have my phone. Anyway. I have something to say to you," he said.

"Sorry for slicing you with a magic sword?" suggested Myra.

"After that," said Rohan. "Although I am sorry for doing that."

"After sorry…" Myra thought about it. "Forgive me? That comes next, after sorry."

"NO!" said Rohan. Though he was laughing now "I wasn't going to say those things. What I was going to say was … I TOLD YOU SO!" He pointed at her. "I told you not to drink the potion! I told you that eating and drinking in Otherland is dangerous. I TOLD YOU SO!" He was now doing a little dance, clanking in his armour boots. "This is my I TOLD YOU SO dance!"

Myra folded her arms. "Huh. You don't have to rub it in."

"Yes I do. I have to rub it in forever. I was right. You

were wrong. You need to do what I say from now on."

"Well, that's never going to happen," said Myra.

Rohan stopped dancing. "Seriously, though. I'm sorry I hurt you. And I'm sorry I left you with the queen to drink that … whatever it was."

"Well, I'm sorry I drank it," said Myra.

"Why did you?" asked Rohan, genuinely curious.

Myra thought about it. She thought about how she'd felt when he walked away and left her with the queen. She thought about the look of horror in Rohan's eyes when he found out it was Myra's fault that the queen stole Shilpa. All these feelings tangled together in her guts, like a nest of snakes. Eventually she found some words. "I think … I was angry at you for being angry at me. But also angry at myself. I just…" She gave up. "Honestly, sometimes I just do things and I have no idea why."

Rohan looked at her with a new expression. Softer. "That sounds really confusing," he said. "But what the queen said about this all being your fault, it's not true. You did something stupid and set fire to a shed. But I know you didn't mean any harm. The queen on the other hand, she *only* meant harm. She set out to steal children. Compared to that, what's a bit of fire between friends?" He laid a hand on her shoulder.

"Ouch." She winced. The cut on her shoulder was

stinging and she was starting to feel woozy. "But …
friends?" she whispered.

Rohan smiled at first, then his look changed to concern.
"Are you OK?"

"I feel … odd," said Myra. Her feet felt very far away,
and her face felt very hot. Then her knees buckled and
she fell.

Strong, perfumed hands caught her.

"She fainted!" Rohan was saying.

"Don't worry, Mab's here," said Mab.

Mab laid Myra on the ground and waved her hands
over her. A moment later she was surrounded by a
glowing ball of light. Myra felt the warmth of it all over
her. It felt like sunshine.

The cut on Myra's shoulder began to close. She could
feel the skin knit back together. She didn't feel any better,
though. Her skin was burning up. It was like the dragon's
fire all over again, but this time it was in her blood.

"There's poison inside," Mab muttered. She looked
at Rohan. "The sword the queen gave you had a poison
tip."

"Can you help her?" Rohan asked, desperate.

Mab kept the spell going. "Shh! I'm working…"

Myra felt a warm tingle through her. She was floating in
the sun, in a pool, like she was on some kind of inflatable.

"Come back," said a voice. Rohan, perhaps?

"Ahhh," said Mab. "There it is. Close to the heart. A drop, just a drop, is enough to end a mortal life. But I'm ever so clever," Mab went on. "I'm the best."

"Less showing off, more healing," said Rohan.

"Who said I can't do both?" said Mab. With a last wave of her hand she pulled Myra gently to her feet.

And just like that, she felt completely well. She stretched her arms up in the warm sunshine and yelled with happiness and relief.

"There. All better," said Mab, with satisfaction.

"And her lungs are definitely working," said Rohan, covering his ears.

Mab clapped her hands in delight. "I did it! I've never saved a mortal from death before! This is exciting!"

Then she looked to Rohan, remembering something. "Hey, I have a bone to pick with you! You broke the spell! I was coming to rescue you but you rescued yourselves. How rude! How's a fairy godmother supposed to get a reputation when her godchildren save themselves?"

"How did I break a spell? I didn't do anything!" Rohan blinked in shock.

"When a mortal knows that an illusion is an illusion, it can be made to shatter," said Mab. "It's one of the few magical things that mortals can do and fairies can't."

Myra laughed. "Isn't it supposed to be me who's good at breaking things?"

"I have hidden talents," said Rohan, looking very pleased with himself, but also surprised.

Mab shook her head. "I can't believe you passed that test, honestly. I thought you were going to go down in flames like a vampire in the noonday sun and I was going to swoop in and save the day."

"The thing is … we're friends," said Rohan, glancing sideways at Myra. "Friends recognise each other, even when they're turned into horrible fire-breathing monsters."

"Yes, we're friends. It's a human thing," said Myra, folding her arms. "You wouldn't understand."

"I understand friendship!" said Mab, frowning. "I have lots of friends!"

Myra and Rohan looked around at the empty clearing. "Yeah. Loads," said Rohan. "They're swarming around you."

"I could do a spell to sew your mouth up, you know," huffed Mab.

"And THAT, right there, is why you have no friends," said Rohan. But then, looking at Mab's hurt expression, he softened. "Except you do have us," he said.

"Are *we* friends?" asked Mab, looking shocked. A green

sparkly tear rolled down Mab's face from her insectile eyes.

"You're crying!" said Myra.

"Awwww!" said Rohan. "You're crying! You like us! You want to be our friend!"

"Fairies don't cry!" said Mab. "This has never happened before. I didn't think it was biologically possible." She wiped away the tear. "I don't even have tear ducts! It must be my magic leaking."

"I think our humanity is rubbing off on you," said Rohan.

"Like a disgusting, soppy plague," said Mab. But a slow smile was spreading over her face. "Come on," she said. "Let's go back to the throne room, my friends, and tell the queen you won the second game."

15

We won ... didn't we?

The throne room was on fire. It was a blue fire that burned without destroying anything. It made the glade look deadly, like a vision of hell, but with more flowers and fluffy pillows.

"Do you think the new interior decor means the queen might be in a bad mood?" suggested Rohan.

"Just a teensy-weensy one," said Myra, showing her finger and thumb half an inch apart.

"But where IS she?"

The room was empty apart from the throne and, of course, the fire.

"Oh, she's here," said Mab. "Somewhere." Mab glanced around. "Just you wait."

Then a drumroll began. Its sound was deep and low, making Myra's entire body vibrate. Her stomach began to churn with the sound.

Another drumbeat kicked in. Faster, higher, with some

kind of snare. And, as an invisible brass section flared into life, the queen appeared, abseiling down from the twilight sky on a gossamer thread.

Her costume, like the wood around them, was on fire, only her fire was a bright red-gold. Her eyes, Myra noticed, were also on fire. That was impossible, but she'd been here long enough to accept that "impossible" wasn't a word that applied to Gloriana.

As the music's beat sped up, woody-rich cellos swelled, and a high flute-like sound picked out a haunting melody, a throng of fairies rushed in from the woods around, screaming.

Or possibly singing, as it was perfectly on the beat.

They surrounded the children, as the queen dropped gently to the ground.

"She might be an evil kidnapping monster with a sick sense of humour," said Myra, "but she REALLY knows how to make an entrance."

"Oh, I know," said the queen. She clicked her fingers and the fairies held their places, forming a circle with the children and the queen in the middle.

"Well," said the queen. "You failed to slay the dragon. What a shame. I get to keep you AND your sister. Victory to me."

"Hang on," said Rohan. "That's not what happened.

You made Myra look like a dragon but she was really herself all along. There WAS no dragon. And you told me to slay the first dragon that came out of that cave. No dragons came out of that cave."

"So he didn't *fail* to slay anything," finished Myra. "In fact, he *succeeded* in breaking your spell!"

The queen glared at them, her flaming eyes looking at them each in turn.

"Are you saying you believe you SUCCEEDED at this trial?"

"Yes," said Rohan.

The queen gave an elegant shrug and clicked her fingers. The flames on her outfit went out and the fabric turned into shimmering water. Her eyes became diamonds. Then she laughed. "It's a fair cop. I'm just messing with you. Congratulations! You won! Round of applause. Well done, you." She narrowed her eyes. "But how did you see through my illusion?"

"It takes more than a couple of scales and a bit of fire to make me not recognise my friends," said Rohan.

"My inner beauty shines through at all times," added Myra.

"Something like that," said Rohan. He looked back to Mab. "Plus, I had some helpful advice. Before the trial, our fairy godmother told us that not everything is as it seems in Otherland."

Mab made an uncomfortable coughing sound. "Er, I wouldn't say I gave you advice as such. I was pretty vague…"

The queen gave Mab a searching look. "Well, fairy godmother? Are you satisfied with what you've done? Helped these humans survive my trials thus far? Risk me losing my changeling? Are you pleased? Do you feel you deserve…" She raised a finger, and it crackled with dangerous lightning. "A reward."

"Don't hurt her!" said Myra, instinctively stepping between the queen and Mab.

"Hurt her?" said the queen. She looked deeply offended. "Do you think I lack imagination? Physical pain is dreary. Only untalented hacks and vampires torture people *physically*."

The queen clapped her hands. "Anyway. Enough bitter talk. We must celebrate! Shake the cobwebs loose before the final game! Lights! Camera! Action!"

With a rush, the space around the children filled with dancing bodies and music and twinkling, pulsing lights.

"Are fairies ever NOT having a party?" groaned Rohan. "It's exhausting."

Myra was going to have a go at him for being no fun, but she realised he was right. Even her bones felt tired.

It was too much. Nothing ever stopped here. There was never peace, never quiet, never the chance to just stand and stare into space gormlessly. It left her brain feeling hyper wired, as though each brain cell might fly off in a different direction, leaving her scattered like a cloud of dust.

Rohan and Myra and Mab were in the centre of a circle of dancing fairies of all shapes and colours and sizes. One had the head of a bull and the legs of an eagle, with talons that looked as though they were made of glass. As it danced, the fairy almost cut Myra's cheek.

"Whoa! Mind where you're waving that!"

The fairy ignored her and continued dancing.

"My *friend* said mind where you're waving that!" said Mab, and swiped the air with a glowing stroke, pushing the bull-headed fairy back.

The fairy snorted and muttered something under its breath.

Myra smiled at Mab. "Thanks."

"Friends don't let friends get maimed by Diamondclaw Fluffshanks!" said Mab.

As the music throbbed, the children couldn't help but dance.

"But no eating or drinking any fairy food," said Rohan firmly.

"Definitely not," agreed Myra. "Though I could murder a burger."

"Your wish is my command," said Mab. "I can fly like lightning to another realm and get you food that's safe to eat. I'll be back!"

She disappeared.

Rohan tapped Myra on the arm. "Look," he said.

Gloriana was at the edge of the clearing, half hidden behind a tree. She was peering into something, muttering to herself. It looked like a tree stump, but it glowed, and shining water sloshed down from the top.

"What's she doing?" Rohan asked.

"Let's go and see," said Myra.

They approached, dodging dancers, and reached the edge of the glade, ducking under tangled knots of branches. The queen was still standing there. She glanced up but didn't appear to see them. Rohan and Myra hid behind a tree, just in case. They heard a snapping twig and a rustle. When they peered round again, the queen was gone.

Rohan motioned Myra to follow, and they crept to the spot where the queen had been. Closer up, the tree stump wasn't a tree stump at all. It looked more like a birdbath, carved out of a living tree. The tree grew around a pool of glowing water, with leaves fanning out around it to form the bowl.

In the water was the image of a small fairy glade. At first, Myra thought it was a reflection of the glade where they were standing, but, she realised, there were no fairies visible. It must be another, empty glade. Sounds of the party hummed faintly from the water.

"Wow," said Rohan. "I think it's like … fairy CCTV. I bet she uses it to spy on her subjects. Though I would've thought everyone was here at this party."

Another sound came through the mirror. Footsteps. Two pairs. Light as cat feet, but distinct. Two pairs of feet walking in little tippy-tappy shoes.

Gloriana and Mab entered the glade together. Mab was looking worried, and was a few steps behind the queen. The queen stopped suddenly in the middle of the glade and turned to Mab.

"She's not going to punish her, is she?" said Myra, worried.

"Shh!" said Rohan.

"What's she going to do?"

"This is as bad as watching TV with my dad. I don't know what's going to happen any more than you do! Just watch!"

Myra elbowed him in the side, but she fell silent and watched.

The queen threw back her cloak and it flapped on a breeze that moved nothing else. "So, Mab. Here we are. My old friend. My former queen. My bitter enemy."

"My queen," bowed Mab. "I slipped away. What happens now?"

The queen didn't reply to this. She inspected Mab, looking her up and down, as though trying to decide something.

"You appear to be very fond of those mortal children," said the queen. "How unfairylike of you. I saw you together, coming through the forest, talking about friendship." She looked up at Mab with big black eyes. "Remember when we used to be friends?"

"Are you growing sentimental, my queen?"

"Never," said Gloriana. "But perhaps YOU are?"

"Never," said Mab. Her voice wobbled, ever so slightly. "The humans mean nothing. My loyalty is to you. My worship is all for you."

"What does she mean, *my loyalty is to you?*" demanded Myra.

"Do you think I'm getting secret subtitles to this? SHH!"

"My queen, I've done exactly as you asked," said Mab in the mirror. "I have obeyed your instructions to the letter!"

"WHAT?" gasped Myra.

"Oh," said Rohan quietly.

Myra felt her stomach fall, down into the dark. Falling forever. They were on their own in Otherland. They always had been.

"Just as you asked, I helped the children survive the first two tasks," Mab went on. "Ready to fail at the final hurdle, in one last dramatic moment of your victory. I know you don't like to stop the story in the middle. You want the game to play out. Always."

"Hmm…" said the queen dubiously. "You didn't do EXACTLY as I asked. I told you that the boy could slay the girl in dragon shape. I even gave him a poison sword to help that along. Only one of them needed to survive to the final, wonderful showdown."

"But, my queen…" Mab blinked and licked her lips. "Then you would only have two changelings, the boy and the sister. Two potential new fairies to worship you. Now you will have three new subjects to praise you and love you. All the kingdom will worship you in your cunning and your showmanship. Your power will be secure for a hundred years. No one can challenge you. Not even me."

The queen looked at Mab and raised an eyebrow.

"I should hope not," she said. "And they suspect nothing? The mortals?"

"Nothing," said Mab. "They think I'm their … friend." Mab made a face that Myra couldn't read. Was she disgusted? Sad? Or some completely inhuman emotion she could never understand.

Because she definitely wasn't human.

Or their friend.

Or their fairy godmother.

16

It's not a betrayal if they never liked you

Mab bowed again. "So will you finally allow me back to court? Not as your queen, of course … but as your Favourite?"

"When the challenge is complete," said Gloriana. "You will be my Favourite for sure." She reached out and stroked Mab's cheek with her long, long fingers. "I cannot WAIT to see those children's faces when they find out that you were always mine. That they were always going to lose."

Then the queen turned to look directly at them, out of the pool. Her eyes bored into Myra's. She smiled with pointed teeth bared.

"No!" Myra cried, splashing at the water with her hand, stumbling backwards. The image cut out. The only sound was the music of the party. Rohan and Myra stared at one another.

"Mab betrayed us," said Rohan.

"No she didn't," said Myra, glaring back at the water for a moment. "She was never on our side in the first place."

Rohan snarled, jabbing his finger at the water. "I should have KNOWN. I never should have trusted her. Who trusts a strange green woman who turns up conveniently after a kidnapping, offering to make everything better? Why am I such an IDIOT?"

"I trusted her too," said Myra. "I wanted to believe her. But there's no such thing as a good fairy, is there?" she said, her face a dark scowl.

"Nope," said Rohan. "No fairy godmothers. Just lying, cheating con artists who used to date our worst enemy."

Rohan was pacing now, running a hand through his hair. "We're done. We're never going to get my sister back now. Mab isn't even going to FAKE help us in the last trial. We're going to lose. We're going to lose."

Myra gave him a ringing slap. He needed it.

"OW!" he objected.

"Panicking isn't going to help anyone," she said. "It's not going to help Shilpa, that's for sure. And it's really annoying." She folded her arms. "We have to win. With or without help. We just need to—"

WHOOMPH!

Mab appeared in a flash of light, holding a steaming

burger. It smelled delicious.

"I got it from the Lost Cave," she said. "Flew as FAST as I could. It's still hot, and a hundred per cent guaranteed not to turn you into a dragon! Wait. Why are you looking at me like that? Do I have something on my face? Have I grown horns? Are horns not in right now?"

"We know," said Rohan. "We know everything."

Mab frowned. "About what?" She looked from one to the other of them, with the hamburger on her palm, little lizard tongue between her teeth.

"We know you're working with the queen," said Myra. "And we know that burger doesn't come from the Lost Cave. You were just in the throne room. We saw everything. You're a liar. We never should have trusted you."

"Oh!" said Mab. Her cat eyes opened wide in shock.

"Oops," came Gloriana's voice from a little way away. The crowd parted to let her through. "Did I leave my mirror on? Did I spoil your beautiful burgeoning friendship?" She covered her mouth, as though embarrassed by her silly, careless, definitely-not-on-purpose mistake. But her eyes were triumphant.

Mab looked to the queen in surprise. "Why did you reveal me now?"

"Plot twist!" said the queen. "Your role is fulfilled. You

146

got them this far. Why does it matter if they hate you now?" She looked more closely at Mab. "You don't … *like* them, do you?"

Mab looked to the floor. The children glared at her.

She said nothing. She looked down at her palm, and the burger disappeared in a cloud of light. "It would've tasted good," she muttered. "And it wouldn't have turned you into a dragon."

"Well? Answer me," said the queen. "You *don't* like them, do you?"

"I worship only you, my queen," muttered Mab. She appeared to pull herself together, and brushed invisible dust from her lapels.

"You see," said the queen, snaking her arm round Mab's shoulders. "My Mab here used to be queen. When her power waned, I became queen. And I had to send her away to teach her some humility. She's been in exile ever since, in the Meantime. Horrible place." She made a face.

"But now I'm back," said Mab, putting her head on the queen's shoulder. "And I'm your Favourite, right?"

"Yes, my very Favourite. It was a good trick you pulled," purred the queen, stroking Mab's hair. "You fooled them so completely."

"I can't believe I thought you were a good fairy," said Rohan.

"There's no such thing as good fairies," said Mab. "Or bad fairies, either. Just fairies."

"No such thing as bad fairies? You were lying to our faces the whole time," said Myra. "I call that bad!"

"I was lying, yes!" said Mab. "But it was all a game, don't you see? All in fun? And if you lose, we can have fun in Otherland forever. In a way, I AM your fairy godmother. I'm making your lives more fun! For eternity!" She gave a smile, showing all her pointed teeth. She looked as though she half expected them to be impressed and pleased. But there was also something sad beneath the toothy smile.

"You're a terrible person and I wish we'd never met," yelled Myra.

The queen burst into laughter. "Oh, their little hurt faces. This IS delicious."

"Delicious," echoed Mab, sounding less than convinced.

"So you played us, just so you could get un-banished?" asked Rohan.

"She was ever so clever," the queen butted in. "As I was passing back from your realm, through the Meantime with my new changeling in tow, back to Otherland, Mab stopped me and suggested that perhaps I could win an even bigger prize if we ran a Knight Game. Three changelings. Of course, I could have just taken her idea and left her there, but I do like a cunning trickster, to keep things exciting. So I promised her a place by my side." She leaned her head on Mab's shoulder. "My Favourite."

"Your Favourite," echoed Mab. "Yours forever."

The queen threw out her arms in a dramatic arc. "We'll play such games, you and I, Mab. We'll have a ball! Literally! Let's have a masked ball to celebrate our victory! We can dance all night!" She took Mab in her arms and waltzed her around, her skirts flaring out in a glittering cloud.

"Brilliant!" murmured Mab as they danced. But was there a flicker of doubt in her eyes? It was so hard to tell.

Giggling, the fairy queen came to a halt and bowed, holding Mab's hand as she did so.

"I hope it's worth it," said Rohan. His eyes bored into Mab. "Spending eternity with HER!" he said, pointing at the queen. "Or at least until she gets cross with you again and throws you out."

Out of the corner of her eye, Myra noticed something. No one else was dancing. The fairy court was silent. Listening. Waiting.

"I still can't believe this was all a trick," said Myra. "We trusted you, Mab."

"I'm a trickster," said Mab with a shrug. "Tricksters

trick. You wouldn't fault a lion for chasing meat, would you? Or a scorpion for stinging?"

"But you're not a scorpion. Scorpions don't pretend to be my fairy godmother then lie to my face," said Rohan. "You're not an animal, you're a person, and you did this to us. You monster."

A flicker of hurt passed over Mab's face. Or it seemed that way to Myra.

"It's not my fault," said Mab. "I had to find a way home. Do you know how boring the Meantime is? I felt myself dying inside. I had to come back." Was that a look of pleading in her eyes? Did she want their pity?

Myra wasn't going to give her any.

"You're worse than HER," said Myra, pointing at the fairy queen. "At least she KNOWS she's evil."

"I prefer 'amoral,'" said the queen coolly.

"Whatever," said Myra.

"Why are you taking this so personally?" Mab blinked. "I just needed something. I used you to get it. That's the way things work here."

"Well then, we're not going to stay here, are we?" said Myra. She turned to Rohan.

"Yeah," he agreed. "We're not staying. Bring on the next challenge. We're going to beat you. And I'm going to take my sister home."

Myra thought he almost sounded as though he believed it.

"Your sister, eh?" said the queen. "Is she really your sister still? Come here, Shilpa. Show your brother that you're almost one of us. That his quest will fail."

The queen beckoned to her left. A small green figure came out of the crowd of fairies. She was dressed in silver and deep woodland green. Her lips were green, her eyes were green. Only her hair was still black, although it had a touch of silver in among the dark curls. When she opened her mouth, her teeth were pointed, as though someone had filed them down. They hadn't, though. She was changing. She was becoming one of them.

Myra felt Rohan stiffen at her side. He let out a horrified gasp. Myra wanted to hug him. But it wasn't something they did, so she didn't.

"We're going to get her back," she whispered to him.

"But what if it's too late?" Rohan whispered back.

Myra didn't have an answer for that.

Shilpa took a little skip towards the queen, and floated a little into the air. Myra noticed something she'd missed before – tiny wings were budding on her back. Not strong or big enough to carry her far through the air yet, but enough to get her off the ground.

She hopped, skipped and jumped towards the queen,

who welcomed her with open arms. Shilpa clambered up the queen's body until she was cradled in the crook of the fairy's elbow. The queen smiled. Shilpa smiled.

Myra and Rohan most definitely didn't.

"Now that your motivation and self-belief is at the lowest possible ebb, let me show you your third and final challenge," said the queen, and raised both her arms, ready to cast some terrible kind of spell. Light flashed. The ground rumbled.

Uh-oh, thought Myra.

17

They like flesh

The earth was shivering beneath their feet. Out of the ground shot a wall, made of mirrored glass and glowing multicoloured light. In a matter of seconds it was towering above them, one hundred feet high.

"Before you is a labyrinth," said the queen. "You must reach the centre." She put Shilpa on the ground and the toddler waved her hands around in fascination. Her magic was beginning to come in. Trails of glitter followed the movement of her fingers. "And when you get there, you must prick your fingers and let your blood flow into the chalice at the centre of a fountain. It's the only fountain in the labyrinth. You can't miss it."

"Blood?" said Rohan. "I don't really like blood. Mine. Other people's. Any blood. Does it have to be blood?"

"It will prove you beat the labyrinth and signal to me to come and get you," said the queen.

"Gross," said Myra. "Can't you just spy on us with your mirror?"

The queen shrugged. "It's how a Knight Game is played and always has been, for hundreds of years."

Myra thought that, for all their flashy games and clever tricks, fairies weren't that imaginative, if they stuck to centuries-old rules.

The queen ushered them forward into the maze, following a few paces behind.

It was like going into a fairground hall of mirrors. Myra could see herself reflected back thousands of times, and Rohan's reflection bounced around behind hers and in front and all around them.

The fairy queen's reflections joined theirs. She was standing behind them. But also all around them.

"You must reach the centre of the maze before the time runs out."

"What time?" said Rohan. The sun here never rose or set. It was always twilight. "What time is it NOW? How long do we have?"

"What time is it?" The fairy queen mimed looking at her wrist. "Three freckles past a hair." She burst into a peal of laughter. "Just kidding. I don't have freckles or hair. Not today. But let's just say you don't have long. So you'd better hurry. And some friends will be following behind you, to keep you tripping along quickly." She pulled something out of her dress pocket. It was the scarab. She pressed its back, and the thing sprouted wings and flew into the air.

Then it split into two.

And into two again.

Then into two more, and more and more until a swarm of flying beetles filled the mirrors around them.

"Better run. They like flesh," said the queen.

The children ran.

"I think we lost them," panted Myra.

They were both leaning against a wall – no longer a mirror, and now only as tall as a human grown-up, except now it was made of something smooth and pink that looked like plastic.

"Unfortunately," panted Rohan, "I think we also lost us. I was trying to keep track of the turns at first but the fear of being eaten alive by beetles took over."

"Well, it's not like we knew where we were going anyway," said Myra glumly. Then her face lit up. She was remembering something. "Unless…" She patted the walls, then leaned closer and sniffed them. "This place looks REALLY familiar. And smells it. Like … gummy strawberry." She turned back to him with a light in her eyes. "Give me a boost? Up the wall."

"What are you—" started Rohan.

"Just do it. I'll explain if I'm right."

Rohan kneeled down and interlaced his hands so she could use him as a step. She stepped and jumped, grabbing the top of the wall and hauling herself up. She huffed and puffed until she was standing on top of the pink wall. She could see a familiar pattern of plastic walls, stretching out around them, though at the edge of her vision there was a fuzziness.

"Can you see the whole labyrinth?" Rohan asked from below.

"No, there's a haze around the edges of this section. But I know how to get to the edge of this bit!" she said.

"How?" asked Rohan.

Myra crouched on the wall then slithered back down, landing heavily and dusting herself down. She grinned.

"We're inside my Princess Mystery Castle!" she said.

"I know what all those words are, but I don't know what they mean in that order," said Rohan.

"I had this castle when I was little!" said Myra. She gestured around her. "It was *the* toy one Christmas – all the other girls had it – and I begged my mum for it. She couldn't afford it but we got it like three years later from a jumble sale and by that time I wasn't into dolls any more. But I took it apart to use the pieces to build a moon base for my Lego astronauts," she explained. "So I know it inside out! It's a toy castle that's got a maze inside! This is what it looked like with the roof lifted off. I lost my roof, now I think about it. I left it on the bus."

"Why did you leave it on the bus? Who takes a roof on the bus?" asked Rohan, blinking. "Oh, never mind that… Why are we in your toy castle?"

Myra looked at him, eyebrows raised. "What part of everything we've gone through here makes you think there's going to be a sensible answer to that?"

Rohan paused and sighed, then seemed to pull something inside him together. He stood up straighter. "So which way?"

Myra pointed left. "That way to the grand ballroom chamber! It's the bit I turned into a subterranean robot repair centre on the moon."

"Of course you did."

So they ran on. Myra led them left, then right, through a large empty plastic bubble full of tall dolls in ballgowns and little Lego astronauts. They were dancing together, and loud pop music filled the air. Myra stopped for a moment as they passed an astronaut dancing on her own. "She's got some moves for someone with arms that only go up and down one way and hands like the letter C."

But they couldn't hang about to watch. After the ballroom they came to a courtyard, with a pink sky and some plastic – but still living – horses, who whinnied at them as they passed. Myra pointed to a doorway. "That's the way out of the castle," she said.

Through the doorway was nothing but darkness.

"The centre of the maze?" said Rohan hopefully.

They ran through the arch into the dark, and came out in a blinding maze of light. Walls zigged and zagged around them, throwing rainbows across their faces.

"I can't tell where the walls begin," said Myra.

"I don't think we're in Barbie's magic Dreamhouse any more…" said Rohan.

Myra held out a hand to discover that the walls weren't solid. Her hand slid into a wall of light and disappeared, making her withdraw it hastily, just in case.

Without discussing it, the children began to walk forward, with their arms outstretched. They might be going towards the centre of the maze, or further away; there was no way of knowing. But there was no logic here, so they might as well go forward.

After passing through several walls, they saw a mushroom growing up from the base of a wall ahead. It was as tall as a toddler and as purple as a bruise. Myra approached it. She stretched out her fingers. Or perhaps her fingers stretched themselves out. When it came to touching things, her hands seemed to have a life of their own sometimes.

Rohan said, "Don't touch it!"

She touched it.

The mushroom started to swell to an even greater, plumper, purpler size, like some monstrous jellyfish taking in a huge breath. Then it breathed out. A storm of spores filled the air in a purple choking mist.

"NO!" cried Rohan.

18
Changed

Myra started to cough. She could feel the spores in her lungs, like a thousand pinpricks of heat.

"If this is deadly poison, I'm going to kill you," coughed Rohan.

Myra was coughing too much to reply.

Then, suddenly, her lungs felt clear. She felt very awake and alert. Rohan was looking back at her, bright-eyed.

"Wow. I think the spores have cleared. How do you feel?" he asked.

"I feel OK," she said. "No, actually, I feel BRILLIANT." She took off down the passage, then ran back. "I feel like I could run for miles. Whatever was in that puffball thing, I don't think it was poison."

"I doubt the queen would booby-trap us with *nice* stuff though," said Rohan. "So there must be something bad in it. Maybe it's like the nectar we drank, and we're going to fall asleep and then wake up as dragons? Or worse…"

He looked down at the shrunken puffball and gave it a wary kick. It was deflated like a balloon at their feet.

"Maybe it wasn't the queen who put it there. Maybe it grows here naturally?" suggested Myra.

"There's NOTHING natural in this place," said Rohan.

They lapsed into silence.

"Well, we can't just stand here," said Myra eventually. "I reckon let's go this way." She pointed towards a passageway with shimmering blue walls. "Just keep moving. Those flying beetle things might find us again."

"I've got to think," said Rohan, shaking his head. "A maze is just a puzzle, right? And I'm good at puzzles."

"Good?" said a voice. "Oh, you think you're SO good, don't you? Or rather ... you wish you were." A small figure was walking towards them. It shimmered green and waddled awkwardly, as though each part of its body was slightly out of time with the rest.

It was Shilpa.

It also wasn't.

She was a fairy now, through and through.

Not a changeling.

Not changing.

Changed.

They were too late.

Her eyes glowed green and sharp teeth nestled between her little green lips. She reached out a hand to point at Rohan, and each finger ended in a pointed claw.

"You're so desperate to be perfect, brother. To keep everyone safe. But you couldn't save me, could you?" She threw back her green head and laughed. It sounded like icy rain. Sharp teeth glinted in her little mouth.

"No, Shilpa," Rohan murmured. His eyes were fixed on the creature.

He looked so impossibly sad, Myra wanted to hug him.

"The thing is, bro," said the thing that wasn't really Shilpa any more. It shrugged its shoulders and let out another little giggle, like glass smashing on skin. "You just need to face the truth. There's nothing special about you. All you can manage to do is to behave yourself well enough that no one pays close enough attention to realise that you're worthless."

"He's not worthless!" said Myra. "He beat the fairy queen's spell and knew I wasn't a dragon. He didn't kill me!"

"Oh, my," said the changeling, its lips curled in a cruel smile. "Is that the best anyone can say about you, Rohan? That you haven't killed anyone lately?"

"That's not fair," began Rohan. Then he turned to Myra. All the colour drained out of his face, leaving him grey. His eyes were hollow, and it made Myra's stomach ache to see how lost he looked.

"Or is it fair?" he murmured. "What DO I do that's worthwhile? If I die today in this labyrinth, are people really going to tell stories about the amazing boy who played Thronehammer according to the rules, and tidied his room, and didn't burn down a shed, and didn't save his sister?"

"That's right," hissed Shilpa. "Now you're catching up with reality. You might as well give up. Lie down. Sleep forever. I can help you sleep." It held out its green hand.

"Don't listen to that thing," said Myra. "It's not your sister." Myra wasn't sure WHAT it was. But it wasn't Shilpa. Not even a little bit.

"No, I'm not anyone's sister now. I am the queen's servant," the green thing agreed. It turned its eyes to Rohan. "And whose fault is that?"

"You leave him alone!" Myra yelled. "Leave my friend alone. You … creepy demon … thing!"

"You want me to leave *him* alone, do you?" said the horrible thing. "As you wish."

The creature that looked like Shilpa faded into a purple mist.

That mist swirled through the air before them and grew, becoming darker and thicker. It formed into the shape of a woman.

A very familiar woman, dressed as a clown.

"Mum?" gasped Myra.

Mrs Duffy blinked her long eyelashes and adjusted her clown nose. Her clown-painted mouth was turned down in disgust.

A pain twisted deep in Myra's gut. Something was horribly wrong.

"Oh, it's you," her mother said. "I was having such a wonderful dream. You were gone, and my life was better." Mrs Duffy was looking at Myra curiously, but without any particular feeling, as though she was an unusual-coloured insect, worthy of mild curiosity and nothing more. "I was walking the red carpet, all eyes were on me. I wasn't weighed down. I was free."

"Mum, what are you doing here?" asked Myra. "Why are you being like this?"

"I'm here to tell you the truth, for once," said her mother. "You remember the day you were born?"

"Obviously not, Mum. I was a baby."

Her mother laughed. For a moment, she seemed herself again. Warm. Silly. Not really like a parent.

"Of course, of course," she laughed. "Well. That day was the worst day of my life. I never wanted to be a parent. I wish you'd never been born."

Maybe that's why she's not like a parent. She never wanted to be. She never wanted me.

Myra stood, mouth open, pink face going white.

"Myra, we should go," said Rohan. "I don't think—"

But her mother wasn't finished. She started to pace up and down, gesturing with her puffy clown sleeves, enjoying the audience.

"Without you, I could've made something of my life, not wasted it on fancy dress and wiping your nose."

She stopped, and her pale eyes bored into Myra. There was nothing behind those eyes. No love. No recognition.

Myra wanted to be sick. She wanted to disappear.

"I could have followed my dreams. You understand, don't you, Myra? You have dreams, don't you?"

"Stop, Mum … please." Myra had never heard her own voice sound so quiet.

"The thing about you, Myra, is that you're thoughtless. You're selfish. A monster, really," said her mother.

Myra felt her throat close up. She couldn't breathe.

"I'm not saying that as a criticism," her mother went on. "I wish I'd had the chance to be myself, too. I could've been a famous actor by now. A writer. A movie director. Not just…" She gestured at her clown costume. "Entertainment at a children's party."

"Mum … please don't say those things. You're my

mum." She felt hot tears coming but she couldn't let them fall. She couldn't let this be real.

"She's *not* saying them," said Rohan slowly. "It's an illusion. YOU're the one saying them, to yourself."

"That doesn't make sense," said Myra. She was lost in her mother's impassive, scornful gaze. It was like falling down a dark hole into a nightmare.

Rohan tugged at her arm, forcing her to look at him instead. "It was that mushroom!" He gestured wiggly lines around his face. "It's making us see things!"

"What?" asked Myra. "She's just a hallucination? But she seems so real!"

Rohan was pacing now, "I think those spores got into our bloodstreams and ... somehow created ... those things."

He waved at the purple-tinged version of Myra's mother. "But the mushrooms didn't make them out of nothing. They're coming from us. All the things that we're scared of."

"Just like you came from me," said her mother. "And ruined my life."

"Just shut up, will you?" said Rohan. "We're having a breakthrough here!"

Myra was slowly trying to piece this all together, through the fog of pain. "Are you saying a mushroom turned all my insecurities … into my mother?" said Myra.

"Pretty much," said Rohan.

Myra shook her head, feeling a kind of wonder. "That's pretty deep," she said. "I don't like it." She fixed her face into a hard expression and pointed at the thing. Her mother. The clown. The illusion. She took a deep breath.

"Get out of here," she said. "We don't believe in you! Go AWAY! You're not real!"

"But … you're worthless. You're a monster!" said her mother, who was decidedly purple by now. "You're a heavy weight round my neck!"

"No I'm not. You're a cloud of mushroom gas, and I'm awesome. GET OUT!"

And, with a pouf, the mushroom-spore-monster-hallucination thing disappeared, leaving only a faintly musty smell and a cloud of purple glitter.

"Dammit," said Myra, stomping her foot. "Why am I so easily fooled?"

"You're not easily fooled," Rohan said. "I was fooled too."

Myra shook her head. "I just… This place makes me feel like I don't know the difference between fantasy and reality, you know?"

"I think, in this place, there isn't that much difference," said Rohan.

"There you go being deep again," sighed Myra. "It's a lot for my brain."

Her brain was saved from dealing with any further wisdom bombs by a chittering sound behind them. Myra and Rohan tensed and clutched on to each other.

"Oh," whispered Myra.

Around them, the maze of light began to fade into a twisted wood.

"The beetles!" Rohan cried.

They began to run along a path through the wood, hopping over tree roots that snatched at their ankles, twisting and turning to drag them down.

The chittering grew closer.

"No! It's got my foot!" Rohan cried, falling into Myra, making her stumble. She fell with a cry. There was a slight thunk as the iron dagger fell out of her pocket. The beetles were coming. She could see their flurried movements.

But then, just as they were about to swarm all over her, they stopped. They hissed.

The dagger was glowing. Myra picked it up as she got to her feet. Instinctively, she held it out at the beetles. They retreated further, curling into little balls of golden shell. She reached out and tapped the closest one with the dagger. It faded into a glistening mist.

"Do it again!" said Rohan.

Myra tapped the next beetle, and the next, and the next ... and each one faded into a glittering nothing.

19

Stealing is awesome!

They both blinked. Then Myra held up the dagger and gestured to it, grinning. "So the moral of this story, kids … is STEALING IS AWESOME!"

"That is so very NOT the moral," said Rohan. "That is never the moral!"

"OK, maybe the moral is let's go now in case they come back to life," said Myra.

They started down the path, hurrying and glancing behind them, but the beetles didn't rise again. Still, they kept going at an almost-run, until Myra needed a rest.

"How did the dagger do that?" she panted as they slowed.

Rohan took it from her and inspected it. It just looked like an ordinary iron dagger.

"Iron! Of course! Any first-level Thronehammer warrior could tell you that. Iron cancels out fairy magic!" he said, slapping his forehead. "Of course! These beetles were created with fairy magic so touch them with iron and they fade!"

"Pretty cool," said Myra.

"So if we come across any more magical monsters, we can use it to protect ourselves," said Rohan, brandishing the dagger like it was a proper sword, swishing it back and forth.

Myra reached up and took it on one of his swooshes. "Yes, but I'm carrying it. I took it. It's mine."

"Sure, whatever," grumbled Rohan. "How DO you still have it, though?"

"What do you mean?"

"I mean, you were turned into a dragon," he said. He gestured to her. "Even if your clothes were transformed with the rest of your body ... if iron stops fairy magic, surely the queen couldn't have transformed your dagger too? So wouldn't it have just been left on the floor wherever you fell asleep?"

Myra shrugged. This was making her head hurt. "Dunno. But I think you're trying to use logic in a land where there isn't any."

"Logic doesn't stop being logic just because fairies don't use it," complained Rohan.

"Well, why don't we worry about why everything's happening when we're so close to actually *winning* this thing. Stop fussing about details," she said.

As far as Myra was concerned, details were like a grey fuzz of boredom that grew on the bones of interesting things. Though, admittedly, it was useful having someone around who didn't find them boring, and could tell her who to stab. "Come on," she said.

They continued along the wooded path until the greenery faded into high walls of polished black stone. There was no hope of climbing to the top of these to look around. As they went on, the path got narrower and narrower.

"There's no way through," sighed Rohan.

"Wait," said Myra. "You said that logic doesn't stop being logic because fairies don't use it?"

"Yeah?"

"What if you're wrong?" she said. "What if it does, here?"

"Huh?" said Rohan.

"What if there IS a way through?" said Myra. "Like through the tree into Otherland, or through the mirror. Come on." She held out a hand to Rohan. He looked at her intently for a moment, then accepted it. And together, they ran into the darkness…

20
Victory!

…And out into a glowing circle of light. Round the edges of the circle rose huge stones, carved into fantastical shapes, like giant chess pieces. In the very centre of the circle was a fountain, tinkling with bright pure water. In front of the fountain stood a table, and on the table was a chalice.

"Rohan," murmured Myra. "We're here! I think we did it. We've won!"

"Not quite," said Rohan. "Remember? The last step?"

They both ran up to the cup. Beside it were two little silver pins. They took one each and pricked their fingers, until a drop of blood blossomed on each of their fingertips. They held their fingers over the cup, until a drop dripped in.

"Throw it in!" said Myra. "Quick!"

Rohan held the cup over the glowing fountain.

"Wait, what if this is the wrong fountain? The wrong

courtyard? This might be another trick?" he said, cup poised.

"JUST DO IT!" yelled Myra. "Stop THINKING!"

He threw the cup into the sparkling water and, as soon as it dropped into the fountain, a sound like a scream ripped through the air. The water in the fountain turned to a beam of pure light, and the scream faded into a golden hum. The beam of light shrank and curled in on itself, becoming a globe, where the fountain had once been.

"What IS it?" asked Myra.

"Your way home," said Gloriana. She was standing at their side. Mab was there too, wearing a new outfit, with green sparkly trousers, platform boots that added an extra foot to her height, and a hat made of black spikes that looked like a deadly weapon.

"The door that will take you home," said the queen. She smiled at them. It was a beautiful smile; a smile that buzzed with the promise of excitement and adventure.

"We ... we've won?" asked Rohan.

"High five!" said Myra, raising her palm, but he left her hanging. He was looking at the queen. Mab was looking at her too, in puzzlement.

"My queen?" murmured Mab. "Why aren't you angry? They've WON!"

"That's a good point. We've won," said Rohan. "Why is the queen happy about it?"

"Never mind why she's happy," said Myra. "Let's get out of here before she changes her mind."

"The girl is right. Don't worry about my feelings," said the queen. "You just need to take your sister and leave. Come, changeling. Or should I say … Shilpa." Little footsteps pattered towards them.

It was Shilpa. No longer green, no longer harsh. She was smiling and her brown chubby cheeks formed dimples of joy when she saw Rohan.

"Shilpa!" He held out his arms to her and she toddled towards him.

"Wait," said Myra. Something about this felt wrong. What if Shilpa turned on him?

But he took her in his arms and cuddled her, grinning. "She's back to normal!" breathed Rohan. He gave her a sniff. "She even smells normal. I mean, her nappy needs changing … but normal."

"Something still isn't right, though," said Myra. Rohan had been all ready to distrust the queen a second ago. But now he had Shilpa, he was ready to be cosy and happy and act like everything was OK.

The queen looked on, with Mab beside her. Mab looked confused. The queen looked triumphant. There was something so wrong with this picture.

"Go on," said the queen to the children. Her smile was fading. She was beginning to look irritated. "Your sister is restored to her former, far inferior self. You've won the game. Why don't you go home? Get out of my sight?"

"No," said Myra.

"But Shilpa!" said Rohan, cuddling her closer. "I have to get her home. Weren't you just telling me not to think so much? To just get on with it? Let's go HOME!"

"Look at her," said Myra. "She's thrilled. She should be turning us into toads in a fit of rage right now. But she's not. She looks like she just won the lottery. There's something wrong here."

"I don't know what the lottery is," said Gloriana. "I don't know what you're talking about." She was still bursting with suspicious happiness, though.

"You're right," said Rohan, hesitating now. He was looking carefully at the queen. "We won, she lost. Why is she happy?"

Then a horrified look passed over his face.

"Oh," said Rohan. He looked from the queen to the portal. "Oh no," he said. He turned to Myra. "She WANTED us to win. She wanted us to open that portal."

"But why?" asked Myra. "What's in it for her?"

"Maybe she gets … power from it somehow? I don't know," said Rohan.

"But I do," said Mab.

She'd been hanging back, uncharacteristically quiet. Now she stepped closer to the portal, inspecting it. She reached out to prod the light with her finger. "It tickles!" she said with a giggle. Then she went on, "That's a direct portal to the mortal realms. The Knight Game opened it. The whole Knight Game was just a cover for a powerful spell I heard of once. It had been at the back of my mind all this time but I couldn't remember it. Fairy memories, never good… The three challenges. A lost thing returned. A dragon defeated. A labyrinth solved. It's a spell of three. The most powerful kind of fairy magic."

She turned to the queen and jabbed a finger at her.

"Oh, clever Gloriana. You wanted to open this portal so you can move freely between the realms. And take as many changelings as you like. Forever. You didn't just want these three changelings. You wanted every human child."

The queen gave a sudden, beaming smile. "Oh, Mab. I can't believe I exiled you for so long. You're the only one who gets me." She went to embrace Mab. But Mab pulled back.

"What is it?" asked the queen. "Are you disappointed that you were able to work out my plan? Not fiendish enough? Look, Mab, I can't help it if my Favourite's ever so clever." She pouted.

"This isn't how it's supposed to work," said Mab. She looked at the glowing ball of light. "We take changelings from time to time. It's a game. And we need them. But this…" She shook her head. "I don't like this. This isn't how the game is played."

"Don't be a fuddy-duddy, Mab, or I might have to exile you again." The queen raised her hands in a menacing gesture, as though she was going to zap Mab there and then.

Mab looked uncertain. "Queen Gloriana…" she started, then trailed off. "I wanted to come home. But I didn't want this."

"This isn't fair," said Myra.

The queen threw back her head and laughed. "FAIR? You still think, with all you've seen in Otherland, that FAIR was ever on the table? All that matters is that I stick to the letter of the law. Fairies have to obey the rules. But we don't have to obey their spirit. I thought you, of all people, would appreciate that, Myra."

"We WON," insisted Myra. "The queen said if we lost, she got three changelings. If we won, we got to go home.

Her getting every human child in the world wasn't part of the deal."

"It wasn't MENTIONED, it's just a happy side benefit," said the queen. She sighed, as though they were all being very stupid. "Don't you see, children? This is what you humans call a win–win situation. You get what you want … and so do I. Everybody wins!"

"Except for the children who get stolen. And their parents. And everyone they know!" said Rohan.

The queen shrugged. "You can't make an omelette without breaking some hearts, isn't that what you humans say?"

"Not even close," said Myra. She stepped in between the queen and the portal. "You have to shut it."

"Why would I do something like that? Through that gateway is an all-I-can-carry changeling buffet. Open every day for a thousand years and a day until this portal fades!" She made a shooing gesture with her hands. "So you might as well go home, and take your dull human sister with you. I don't need you now I have all the children I want."

Myra realised something. There was a hungry look in her eyes. Why was she so keen to get rid of them? She and Rohan exchanged a glance.

"Why do you care if we go home?" asked Rohan.

"Makes no difference to me whatsoever if you stay or go. But your parents will be wondering where you are."

"Why do you care what our parents think?" said Myra. "That's not very fairylike of you."

"She WANTS us to go," said Rohan.

Then Myra knew the answer. For once. "I don't think the spell will work if we don't go home, will it?" she said slowly. "The Knight Game isn't finished until we claim our prize and go home."

"Nonsense," said the queen. "But perhaps I should help you move along. You're boring me."

The queen looked far from bored. She looked like a cat right next to a mouse that was close to its hole.

"No matter," said Gloriana. "I can force you through." She raised her hands to cast a spell. "As long as you go through and claim your prize, the bargain is complete. Whether it's voluntary or not."

Myra's heart began to flutter. She had to do something.

With a little flash of glitter, Mab transformed her outfit. She smiled. "Ooh, I do love this dress. It has pockets."

What was she doing? Trying to distract the fairy queen so she didn't push them through? Well, all she was doing was managing to distract Myra.

Focus, Myra! What can I do against fairy magic? And why is Mab going on about pockets?

Myra's own hands were at her sides, fists balled in helpless anger. Just then her finger brushed against her pocket.

Oh!

It's not the pockets. It's what in them.

She slipped her hand inside. *What can I do to stop the queen? I can break things.*

Iron.

Iron will break it.

She drew the dagger from her pocket and stabbed it into the heart of the glowing sphere, feeling magic judder through her arm and flood her body, making her feel like she was about to explode.

"NO!" yelled the fairy queen.

Then another scream ripped through the air. The orb itself was screaming, louder and louder, until she thought her eardrums might burst. A wall of power hit her square in the chest and she was thrown backwards. She scrabbled to her knees to see the ball of light collapse in on itself with a WHOMP and a hiss.

The portal was closed.

There was silence for a moment.

The queen's eyes lit up red, and a long serpent's tongue whipped out between her lips. She flicked her wrist and Myra found herself floating into the air. Rohan was beside her. Mab too. They were bound in chains of light, which felt both hot and freezing at Myra's wrists and ankles. Something was bound round her mouth, so she couldn't speak. She looked at Mab and Rohan. Their mouths were hidden behind what looked like silver cobwebs.

"I don't need to hear any more from any of you," said the queen. "You've closed my portal. And I can't tell you how much that ticks me off. But by doing so, you've stopped yourselves from ever going home. Your parents will never know what happened to you. I can take some comfort in the chaos that you've caused. And I can start work on transforming Shilpa into my changeling once again."

She beckoned Shilpa to her. The toddler looked up, fear in her dark eyes. She was rooted to the spot in terror.

The queen gave a noise of disgust and shot out a rope of light, snagging Shilpa round the toddler's plump middle and whipping her towards her. Shilpa let out a terrified cry.

Myra tried to yell, but no sound came out. She could see Rohan straining to cry out, his eyes full of pain.

"Well now," said the queen. "Until I decide what to do with you three, you're going to prison. The traitor and the mortals. What WILL I do with you? Well, I know I'll have fun deciding, that's for certain. Bye for now!"

The queen raised her hand, propelling her prisoners through the air in their glowing chains, faster and faster, into a pure darkness.

21
Behind iron bars

Their cell was suspended in a woodland glade. It was less a cell and more a cage, with shining bars decorated at the top and bottom with flourishing carvings of leaves and animals. As prisons went, it was rather attractive. The queen couldn't resist stylish touches, even in her punishments.

Their bonds melted after a while, and they could move and talk again.

"Well, this is not looking good," said Rohan, nursing his jaw.

"Maybe I shouldn't have helped you close that portal," said Mab, staring out through the bars. "Then we would have all been better off, and Shilpa would be no worse off."

Myra looked up at her. "Why *did* you help me remember that I had the iron dagger in my pockets? If you're on her side."

"I did more than help you remember," said Mab. She looked insulted. "I put the dagger in your pocket in the first place. Didn't you wonder how it got there? After you were turned into a dragon?"

"I did!" said Rohan. He pointed to Myra. "She didn't, though."

"Well, it was meeee!" said Mab. She held up her left hand. "Haven't been able to do magic with this hand since I touched that dagger! I hope I get the power back eventually. I like that hand. It's one of my two favourites."

"I don't get it, though," said Rohan. "You're working for the queen. Why the sudden change of heart? If you even have a heart."

"I don't, actually. But I just... I felt..." Mab shrugged and continued staring out through the bars. "I'm not entirely sure what I am. I think all those years in the Meantime broke me. Or maybe it's you two." She looked back at them, suddenly angry. "I could've been Gloriana's Favourite. Given time, I probably could've worked my way back up to being queen again myself. But ever since you two arrived, ever since I got back to Otherland, I've been ... off. I started out thinking I was just playing along, pretending to be your fairy godmother. But you two..." She shook her head. "I think humanity's contagious. Like a disgusting disease. I caught feelings from you."

"You can't CATCH feelings, Mab," said Rohan. "I think you're just a better person than you gave yourself credit for."

"Yuck," said Mab. "Goodness. So human. And now the queen's probably going to banish me again. But you know the worst thing?"

"What?"

"I don't even care. I don't care what happens to me." She put a hand on her chest. "To ME! The most important person in the world. In fact, I'm GLAD I did it! It felt good. It felt … right!"

She sighed heavily.

"It's no use. I'm broken." She sank down to her knees in despair. "I'm practically a mortal now."

Myra reached out and patted her back carefully, to avoid squashing her wings. "You're not broken. You helped us."

"Plus, you helped save all the children on Earth from the queen," added Rohan.

"So … I'm a hero?"

Mab brightened. Myra and Rohan exchanged glances, then shrugged.

"Sure," they said together.

Mab grinned. "Maybe I can work with that!"

"And you know what heroes do?" said Rohan. "They

help their friends break out of cages, rescue their sisters, and get home."

"That's a very specific take on being a hero," pointed out Myra.

"Well, it's the hero we need right now," said Rohan.

"Ah," said Mab. Her face fell. "In which case, I may not be a hero after all." She gestured to the bars of the cage. "Any counterspell I do won't be powerful enough to break us out of here. Especially not one-handed. I've had years without doing magic, so I'm nowhere near as strong as the queen now."

Myra felt deflated. Were they really trapped in this cage? And in Otherland? Forever?

"I wonder what the queen will do now?" said Myra. "I mean, apart from probably torture us forever."

Myra felt a giggle try to wiggle up her throat when she said "forever". It was a ridiculous idea. Forever.

She looked at Rohan, and he looked back, worried. "You OK?" he asked.

"I'm just … thinking … you might be the only other human being I ever see," she said.

"Well, how do you think I feel? I'll have to look at YOUR FACE for the rest of my life," said Rohan.

"Mate, have you seen YOUR face?" she returned, but they were both smiling.

Myra felt it was one of those smiles that might crack into tears at any moment, so she bit her lip.

"I'm glad you're insulting each other," said Mab approvingly. "I was worried that being good meant never calling anyone names ever. That would be worse than death. Though death MIGHT be what the queen has in store, now I think about it."

They descended into silence for a moment.

Myra inspected the bars of the cage, giving them a tug. Then she turned to Rohan.

"Hey, if we can get out of the cage, I think I've got an idea for how to rescue your sister. You know how you said it's still our birthday back home, so the portal's still open? I mean, the one we came here through, in that blue tree in the Meantime."

Mab nodded.

"OK," said Myra. "Then can you get hold of some nectar or ambrosia?"

"Easy. It literally grows on trees in Otherland." She looked at Myra. "Are you planning what I think you're planning?"

"If what you think I'm planning is you turning me into a dragon, then yes!" said Myra.

"Yessss!" said Mab, clapping her hands. "I can do that! I have enough magic for that kind of illusion, even on my worst day." She held up a finger in warning to Rohan. "But don't look at Myra while she's transformed. You know it's her, so you seeing through the spell will break it. Like you did when she was a dragon before."

"Noted," said Rohan. "No looking at Myra. Though why I'd want to look at HER face anyway is a mystery."

"Mate, I think you mean YOUR face," said Myra. "Anyway, when I've scared the fairies away, as a dragon, I can grab Shilpa," she went on.

"Won't you hurt her?" said Rohan. "Just ... I'm flashing back to you as a dragon, stumbling around breathing fire with all the precision of a home-made nuclear bomb."

"Hey! I was new to it!" objected Myra.

"Still, I think I should grab her while the fairies are distracted by dragon-you."

"Fine, fine," said Myra, a little grumpily. "You hog all the glory while I do all the work."

"She's *my* sister," reminded Rohan. "I should be the one to rescue her."

"I hope she has a full nappy when you do," said Myra.

"I do love it when mortals bicker," grinned Mab. Then her face fell. "Oh. It won't work. Your dragon plan won't work."

"Why?" said Myra, bristling. "Are you saying I'll mess it up?"

"I just don't think anyone will fall for the illusion. You see, a fairy could tell a real dragon from a fake one right away."

"Can they sense the magic of the spell?" asked Rohan.

"No, they can sense the stink of its smell," said Mab. "Or rather, the absence of stink. Real dragons smell TERRIBLE. Like a stable that hasn't been cleaned for four hundred years. You didn't know that when Myra was turned into a dragon, because you've never smelled a real dragon."

"Either that, or Myra smells like one already," said Rohan, getting a dead arm from Myra for his trouble.

"So turning you into a dragon won't do any good," said Mab.

"Oh," said Rohan. "Turning her into a DRAGON won't do any good but… Can you use ambrosia to turn people into other things? Not just dragons?"

"Of course – if you pick the right flower," said Mab.

"Then I've got an idea for something else we could turn her into," he began. "Something worse than a dragon."

The others leaned closer and he told them his plan.

22

Who's who?

"So, in summary, that MIGHT work ... except for the fact that I can't get us out of this cage," said Mab.

"Maybe you can't," said Myra. "But I think maybe Rohan and me can."

"Rohan and I," corrected Rohan.

"Are you seriously grammar-checking my escape plan?"

"Life-or-death situations are no excuse for using the wrong parts of speech," sniffed Rohan. "But go on. How can we get out of here?"

"Well, Mab was just saying you'll break the ambrosia spell if you look at me while I'm transformed into a dragon or whatever?" She gestured to the bars. "What about if we do that here?"

"I AM looking at the bars," said Rohan. "I've been looking at them for ages. They're still there."

"It's not just about looking, though, is it? You only turned me back from being a dragon because you saw who I really was."

"So what are these bars really? A spell? We knew that. They're magical bars." Rohan stared at the bars, willing them to melt away.

"Yes," said Myra. "But to really see through them, you've got to look at what they're NOT."

"You're not making sense," said Rohan.

"They're iron bars," said Myra. She gave them a tug. "Except that's impossible. Because fairies can't do magic on iron. They can't be iron. So they can't be here at all…"

As she said it, she fell forward, her hands clutching on nothing, landing with a thump on the moss below. She rolled over painfully and looked up at where she'd been imprisoned a moment before.

Rohan and Mab were now just standing on an open platform, floating in the air and staring down at her in surprise.

"I broke the spell," she groaned. "I think I might have also broken my bum, though."

Why did I have to get good at logic the one time it was going to make me fall off something?

Mab took Rohan round the waist and flapped her wings, floating them down to the ground. Myra was on her feet, wincing slightly as she checked herself for broken bones. There didn't seem to be any, but there was a lot of soreness.

"That was awesome!" Rohan flapped his hands in excitement. "You broke the spell! It's magic! You did magic!"

"Nah," said Myra. "I used logic." She puffed out her chest. "Now, let's turn me into something nasty!"

The next few minutes involved a lot of Mab disappearing into bushes, pulling off flowers, sniffing them, then throwing them away. "Nope, that one turns you into a troll. Hmmm … no, a pig. Definitely don't want that one. Honestly, I don't know why this one even exists. Why would anyone want to turn themselves into an aubergine?"

As they fell, each flower grew again into a new plant. When she finally found the right one, she waved a hand over it and motioned to Myra to take it.

"Squeeze the nectar on to your tongue," said Mab.

Myra did. It was even more delicious than the nectar that had turned her into a dragon. And much faster-acting. She felt her body shift and change in a matter of seconds…

Myra peered through the bushes. The throne room was full of fairies having a party. It was a slightly less exuberant affair than the last one Myra had been at. There was music, sure, and the fairies were dancing wildly, but the music sounded like an unwound music box, and the dancing fairies glanced around themselves, nervous and jittery. In the centre, in a throne made of glass and ice, the queen looked listless, and her mood was catching.

"Dance harder!" commanded the queen. "You're dancing with all the rhythm of vampires!"

The fairies began to thrash to the music, obeying the queen's command. The music itself changed, growing wilder and deeper. The queen smiled, ever so slightly. She rose to her feet and began to dance herself, swooshing her golden skirts from side to side in time to the music. It was a mesmerising sight. Myra felt that she'd never seen true dancing until that moment. Watching the queen move to the music, it felt like seeing music in human – or at least humanoid – form. Myra wondered, could the queen really be evil? She moved like something heavenly. Like poetry. Myra didn't even LIKE poetry! And yet … this was pure beauty.

Then, in one flowing motion, the fairy queen bent down and pulled a little figure into her arms. Shilpa.

The queen began to throw her into the air in time to the beat. She danced through the crowd, with Shilpa swooping up into the air and back down again. Each time she went up, Myra's heart clenched. Usually Shilpa loved being thrown up by grown-ups – but gently, and just a little. Myra saw her face for a moment as she descended. She was terrified. Each time the queen caught her, her nails dug in to Shilpa's soft skin. Myra knew this would be even worse for Rohan, wherever he was hiding.

The queen soon grew bored with the game. She put Shilpa down upon the floor, allowing her to toddle away in between the dancing legs. Perhaps Myra could grab her now? No. She had to stick to the plan.

There was a first time for everything.

Now. Go on, Myra, she thought. *Don't mess this up...*

The fairies turned to see a figure striding into the party, from the bushes at the edge of the woods. Gold skirts rustled around her as she walked.

She approached the band. She climbed up on to the stage.

A whisper went through the party.

The figure stage-dived, hurling herself on to the waiting crowd, whose whispers became yells and howls of delight and confusion.

The stage-diving figure sailed across the top of the crowd, the fairies moving her hand over hand, some using magic to propel her along.

Until she reached a gap in the crowd, where a banquet

was spread. In the middle of the banquet was a giant cake.

The figure went feet first into the cake, knocking it over, covering all the nearby fairies in clouds of frothy icing. The other fairies erupted into cheers.

"The queen! The queen! The queen!"

Myra smiled. She could get used to this. The chanting. The cheers.

Don't get distracted, she thought.

After all, she wasn't the only queen in the room. The real Queen Gloriana was striding towards her, in the same long, gold puffy dress.

The queen looked at Queen Myra in fascination. "Well. I AM quite something, aren't I?" she said. She bowed to the newcomer. "I haven't had a visitor this attractive since Amelia Earhart crashed her plane into Otherland." She looked the other queen up and down. "You're better dressed than her, of course."

"Never mind my outfit," said Queen Myra. "You should bow before your queen."

The queen laughed, like a thousand tinkling bluebells in a poisonous shower of rain. "I think you'll find *I* am *your* queen. Whoever you are, this disguise is very flattering. But perhaps you've taken it quite far enough for now. Return to your true shape, fairy."

"I won't," said Queen Myra. "You can't make me."

"I beg to differ," said the queen. "Except I never beg."
She raised a hand to cast a spell and waved it at Myra.

Nothing happened.

"That should have worked. That spell could reveal
even the most powerful fairy's true shape," said the queen.
Her lizard tongue shot out and licked her dark-green
lips. "Unless you're a—" She suddenly went stiff. "THE
MORTALS HAVE ESCAPED! CAPTURE THEM!"

"Yes, we have," said another voice. A third queen stood
in the middle of the party. "We're here for my sister. Oh
look, here she is."

Myra tried not to look at the fourth queen, who picked
up Shilpa and handed her to the third queen.

"Four queens!" a fairy squealed.

"Which one's which?" cried another.

"Don't you recognise your queen?" said the real queen,
snatching Shilpa from Queen Rohan. Her tone was
white-hot fury.

"I am your queen!" yelled Queen Rohan. "Capture the
others! They're the fakes!"

"No, YOU'RE the fake!" cried Queen Myra.

Rohan gave her a look and muttered, "Not helping…"

"How can we tell who's real?" asked Robin Goodfellow
in a squeaky voice.

"I'm the real queen, you grogwits!" cried the queen.

The mob of fairies hesitated, looking between the queens. Between three of them. The fourth at the edge of the trees now. She was carrying something in her arms. Some*one*. She was running for the blue forked tree.

"That one's getting away!" someone cried.

"Which one?"

All was chaos. Fairies howled and flew, and queens ran and flew.

"Give me the child!" snarled Queen Rohan.

"Never. She's my changeling, you faker!" cried the real queen.

"Give ME the child," said Queen Myra. "She's mine!"

The crowd was gradually drifting towards the blue forked tree. One queen was already there. She was carrying Shilpa in her arms.

"TWO changelings," said the real queen. Her eyes grew wide. She looked down at the child in her arms. "How do I know if I have the real one?"

"I'll give you a hint," said Queen Rohan. "Yours is melting." He took the other Shilpa from the other queen and kissed the top of Shilpa's head.

The true queen looked down at the child in her arms and saw it melt away to nothing.

"Come on!" Queen Myra shoved Queen Rohan – in his own shape now, though still wearing a golden dress – into the blue tree, with Shilpa in his arms. The other queen followed him.

Myra took the dagger out of her skirts and stabbed it into the base of the tree. It started to hum with power, and she pushed through the tree into the dark.

The sounds of Otherland were gone. The screaming fairies, the music, and the powerful, intoxicating smells all faded into silence and blackness.

23

The final queen

Before Myra had been to Otherland, she hadn't realised quite how drab the Meantime really was. Everything shifted, nauseatingly. Nothing sparkled. She felt a deep, damp sadness for a moment.

A few feet away she saw Rohan, with Shilpa in his arms. His fairy dress was fading now, and his dark suit was peeping through, although the tie was long gone.

"Rohan! Is Shilpa OK?" Myra called.

As Rohan saw her, he smiled and waved with his free hand. "Fine!" He clearly didn't want to put Shilpa down now he had her.

As he looked right at her, she felt herself begin to shrink, and her golden dress turned into a bright-green tutu, wellies, and – looking down at herself, she saw – a T-shirt saying NOW PANIC AND FREAK OUT. Myra ran over and took Shilpa from him, giving her a squeeze.

"Fine, care about ME being OK after you shoved me

through a tree," said Rohan, but he couldn't help smiling back.

"Tree!" said Shilpa. "Smooshy tree!"

"It was a smooshy tree," said Myra. "And you're a smooshy baby!" She turned to Rohan. "Look, she's hardly green at all. Will it fade, Mab?" She looked at the remaining queen, who was dusting down her golden dress. As Rohan and Myra looked at her, she didn't change.

She looked right at Myra and gave her a smile she didn't like one bit. "Hello, mortals," she said. She was standing straight and tall, her golden dress flapping in a breeze. "I'm afraid you've made an error," she said. "You left your other friend back in Otherland and brought me with you."

Myra's insides turned to ice.

Then the queen began to laugh. It didn't sound like tinkling bells or falling icicles. It was a warm laugh, though strange. The queen began to fade, her golden dress began to turn into a green jumpsuit with silver shoulder pads. It was Mab, laughing herself sick.

"Your face!" she squeaked, unable to get the words out properly, she was laughing so much. "Your FACES!" she said, pointing at Rohan and Myra, with one finger outstretched at each. "I had you! I fooled you! You really thought I WAS the queen."

"That was so MEAN!" said Myra. But she started to laugh too.

Rohan joined in too. So did Shilpa. It was a good sound to hear. A little gurgling plump toddler laugh, becoming a snotty snort at the end.

"Does anyone have a hanky?" asked Rohan hopefully, seeing the snot drip down his sister's upper lip.

Myra wiped Shilpa's nose on her tutu.

"Gross," said Rohan.

He turned to Mab. "Hey, how come you didn't change when I looked at you? That's what made me think you really were the queen!"

"I was doing the spell on myself," said Mab, stroking her cheek with her slender fingers. "First-hand spells are more powerful. You'd have to look at me for at least a minute to break a first-hand spell. I mean, obviously, that would be a treat for you. But rather time-consuming."

"Good to know for the future," said Rohan. "Though hopefully I won't ever have to break a fairy spell again. I just want to go home."

Myra agreed. Before today, she might have said there was no such thing as too much excitement, but she felt a sudden, powerful urge for a nice quiet sit-down and a biscuit. Not even an exciting biscuit.

Mab let out a whistle. "Let's go. Time to get you two

home. And me to anywhere but here."

The air filled with the sound of flapping wings. The strange birds were swooping down towards them.

With a little shoving and panting, they were all on the backs of the birds. Mab was too worn out from her spells to fly them on to the birds.

Rohan, Shilpa and Myra shared a bird, while Mab had one to herself.

Rohan ruffled Shilpa's dark hair and pulled her closer to him, safe in his lap, and she made a sleepy noise. "Nearly home," he whispered to her.

"Are you tired?" yawned Myra. "I am TIRED. I don't think I've ever been this tired. Except maybe the time I lost my aunt's cat and had to wander around all night with a pocket full of fish trying to tempt it home."

"Did you really put fish in your pocket?" asked Rohan.

"Actually, it was your pocket," said Myra. "It was the pair of trousers I borrowed after dropping custard on mine at our party last year."

"Never give them back," said Rohan.

They fell into silence and watched the strange landscape beneath them. They went over the Sea of Abandoned Dreams, over a grey field full of what might have been ghosts, or might have been grey candyfloss. After Otherland, the place seemed like nothing and nowhere.

Myra could see why Mab had wanted to escape it so much.

Apparently Rohan was in the same mental groove.

"I wonder what Mab will do now," he said to Myra.

"She could come and live with me," said Myra. "I don't think my mum would mind."

"I'm not sure even your mum would put up with you bringing a green stranger home to live."

"Maybe you're right," said Myra. "She didn't like it when I invited the crossing guard to live with us when I was six. And she wasn't even a magical creature. Oh, look! I think we're here!"

They were flying above the black sand beach, where they'd first appeared in the Meantime.

"DOWN!" called Mab.

The birds dive-bombed down, and the children braced for impact. But this time the birds touched down as gently as feathers, and melted into the sand.

"Bye-bye, birdies," said Mab, a little sadly. She picked up a single feather from the ground. "I think without me in the Meantime to keep them whole, they were starting to fade."

"I'm glad we only found that out when we were safely on the ground," said Rohan.

"So," said Myra. "How do we get home?" She looked

around the beach. There was nothing close by, just empty black sand and clear water stretching out into the distance.

"We use the mirror, of course. It's always mirrors in and out of the mortal realms." Mab shook her head. "Keep up!"

"What mirror, though?" asked Rohan.

There was nothing there.

Mab pointed at the sea. "That giant one right in front of your nose, sillynoo! Have you ever seen a shinier mirror?"

They all approached the edge of the sand and looked into the still water. Their faces stared back up at them. Myra, Rohan, Shilpa and Mab, all gazing back up from the sea. It really was a perfect mirror.

"Come on! Let's hurry things along. I want to get out of this tedious place! I've had QUITE enough of it for at least twelve lifetimes," said Mab. Quickly, she reached down, picked up Shilpa, and threw her into the sea.

"NO!" shrieked Rohan, and dived in after her.

"Thought that would speed you up," said Mab. "Now you too," she said to Myra.

Myra gave one last look at the shifting grey place and, with a shiver, dived into the water.

Strings of sticky stuff pawed at her skin. She was down

in thick darkness, enveloped.

She couldn't breathe. She couldn't feel. She was nothing.

24

Home

Then, in a moment, she was back in Shilpa's bedroom, right where they'd started. Shilpa was sitting on the carpet, on the exact spot where she'd disappeared.

"Home!" said Shilpa, and started to wriggle on her bum.

The clock on the wall said ten o'clock. Morning? Night? Myra looked to the window. She could see the moon in the sky. That answered that.

"Sticky!" Shilpa giggled, rubbing her fingers over her face. "Sticky sticky sticky!"

Myra turned to the mirror. "Where's Mab?"

There was a moment's silence, then two greenish hands emerged. They pressed at the frame of the mirror, but no figure emerged at first. Then, slowly, Mab's head, with its pointed ears and – currently – spiky silver hair, popped out through the glass of the mirror. The glass bent and pooled outwards like the surface of a very thick liquid.

Then, finally, she shot out of the mirror and fell to the floor in a heap.

Behind her, the mirror made a shlurping noise, then became still. A normal mirror once again.

"That was close!" said Mab. "The gate was closing on me! I almost didn't make it through! Time in the Meantime's more like human time. We must have caught up with the night. Or the night caught up with us. Anyway. Here now. Phew." She shook her head, and as she did so, she began to change. Her green skin turned a more human brown, her eyes grew smaller and her ears more rounded. Though they still kept a slight point at the tip. Her eyebrows grew thicker and darker. She looked – if you didn't look too closely – almost human. And a little like she could be related to both Rohan and Myra. She kept her spiky silver hair, however, and if you DID look closely, there was something very glittery about her. She kept her wings, too, but snapped her fingers and suddenly she was wearing a long flowing coat, which only gave a hint of something underneath.

"Now I'm in exile, I need to go undercover," she explained. Then, with a wave of her hand, a pair of sunglasses appeared. She put them on.

"It's night-time," said Rohan.

"Indoors," added Myra.

"All the more reason why wearing these will make me stand out," said Mab.

"But aren't you supposed to be undercover?" said Rohan.

"Yes, as a human. But as a COOL human," said Mab. She looked around the room. "This is where you live? It's very small."

"This is just my sister's room." Rohan glanced to the door. The house was eerily quiet in the near-darkness.

"Where is everyone?" asked Myra.

"Wait, there's a quick way to check." Rohan got down on his knees, looking for something. "I must have dropped it when we found Shilpa," he said. "Ah, there." He picked up his mobile phone. "Aaaand … yup. Here it is. With about a million missed calls." He looked at his phone screen. "They're out searching for us. They've probably called the police. They've probably called ALL the police in the country. The house is probably surrounded by armed guards right now." His voice was taking on a note of panic.

Just then, the door slammed. He heard voices downstairs. Rohan's father, saying, "Let's try his friend Mark's house next. Remember, the officer said he'd probably be with a friend."

"But would he have taken Shilpa? Why would he do

that? And why did he leave his phone behind?" came Rohan's mother's voice. She sounded drained and tired and on the verge of tears.

"I bet my mum's just gone home," whispered Myra, with a little hollow feeling growing inside her. "She probably isn't even worried. Why don't I go downstairs first? I can be your human anger shield."

Rohan swallowed. "No. I've got to do this. I've faced a dragon and a fairy queen, not to mention a mushroom made out of my own insecurities. I can face my parents."

"Well," said Mab. "I think that's my cue to leave. Everyone is safe home. No need for me to stay around for the tears and human nonsense."

Footsteps were climbing the stairs. Mab bowed to the children.

"Time for me to disappear into the night and find my new life, leaving you to pick up the pieces," said Mab. "Farewell, children. Until the next time. If you want me, just say my name three times into a mirror. Or any reflective surface will do. But I prefer mirrors. They make for far more stylish an entrance. No one wants to materialise out of a muddy puddle."

"Mab, we—" began Rohan.

But Mab wasn't listening. She threw open the window, hopped on to the windowsill, flared out her wings, and swooped away into the night. For a moment, she was outlined against the moon. Then she was gone.

The footsteps reached the top of the stairs.

"Before you say anything, Mum, we're OK," Rohan began, as the door opened.

But it wasn't Rohan's mum in the doorway. Mrs Duffy was standing there, still in her clown outfit, her make-up smudged all over her face. She'd been crying. Apparently for hours.

"MYRA!" she yelled, and grabbed Myra into an enormous hug. "My Myra! You're OK! You're OK!"

"Yes," said Myra. She nuzzled into her mother and soaked up the hug like it was sunshine. "I am. I am."

Rohan's parents squeezed through the doorway, round the hugging Duffys. Rohan's mum grabbed Shilpa up, squeezing her tight, and his dad gave Rohan a slightly more modest hug. "You're safe," he said. "Oh. I'm so relieved."

"Where WERE you?" said his mother. She clutched Shilpa as though she'd never let go of her ever again.

"Queen?" asked Shilpa, taking a fistful of her mother's hair.

Rohan's mother leaned in to Shilpa. She sniffed slightly, and frowned in confusion. "You smell … different," she said.

"What happened?" said Rohan's father. He looked to the open window. "Why is the window open? Can you explain what on earth is going on? Where have you been?"

"Sorry," said Rohan. "I'm so sorry, everyone. Shilpa ran off – she was scared by the fire when she woke up – and we chased her and then we lost track of time. Then we got lost. And I dropped my phone when I was running after Shilpa."

"Sorry," said Myra. "We didn't mean any harm."

"Well, I look forward to explaining that to the police," said Rohan's dad. He sighed deeply. "But I'm just glad you're all safe."

"Let's go downstairs and have something to eat and drink," said his mother. "Explanations can wait until you're all fed."

"We'll talk about punishments later," said Mrs Duffy, looking as stern as she could in her smudgy clown make-up. "You scared me so much, Myra Duffy! What would I have done if you'd been … gone?" She looked at Myra and grabbed her again into the biggest hug. Myra could hardly breathe. But she didn't care. Oxygen was for losers. "Now, let's get you downstairs and get you fed. But you'd better know, things are going to change around here. And I don't think you're going to like it." Again, the stern look.

Or as stern as a smudged clown can look.

As she followed her mother downstairs, Myra thought that, actually, maybe, she *was* going to like it.

"What are you grinning at?" whispered Rohan.

"She's going to punish me. I think she's going to start being stricter!" said Myra dreamily.

"And you're happy about that? Weirdo," said Rohan.

But Myra smiled to herself. The creature in the maze had lied. Her mum cared about her. She wanted her there.

And Myra was going to have the punishments to prove it.

Acknowledgements

This book began a very long time ago, in a very different form, so the list of people who helped it come into being spans 20 years and more.

To my wife, Karen, thank you for being there through so many iterations of this book, always ready to help me brainstorm a tricky bit, and walk the dog when it wasn't your turn when I was on a deadline.

To Tom, my editor, and George, who drew the wonderfully bright, weird cover, thank you for shaping the world of Otherland with me. To Tom specifically, apologies for the emotional scarring caused by melting babies.

To the whole Nosy Crow team – thank you for your support across many books, but especially for this one as it's so close to my heart. And happy tenth anniversary to the Crow's Nest! This book contains no crows but it does have ravens made out of memories of other birds, so I imagine there's some crow in the mix there somewhere.

Thanks to Polly Nolan, for making this book and many others possible.

To Vanisha, for insights, critiques and questions.

To Amy McC and Kirsty A for thoughtful comments

and encouragement.

To the book's earliest supporters, Anna Power, Rick Mason and Ben Morse – whose Hackney Salon gave a very early draft its first airing. Thank you. This is not the book you knew, but it carries a piece of its soul.

To my parents, thank you for giving me so many worlds to explore, through books and in woods and fields.

To the Girls, for being there from the very beginning, cheering me on.

To Mac, Onika and Milla, for showing me early in life that friends can be family and that creativity flows wild through all of us in so many ways.

To Diane Purkiss, thank you for teaching me just how troublesome fairies can be. (To everyone else with an interest in fairies, read Diane's book!)

To Imogen Russell-Williams, thank you for the walks and the rants.

To the puppies, for voice notes, dog pics and badgers.

Team Swag, I cannot possibly thank you all enough. The best invisible friends a writer could ever hope to have.

To Molly, thank you for believing in me.